DOUBLE ALCHEMY

Clear Star Romance
1

Stephanie
Ascough

Double Alchemy
February 2024.
Copyright © 2024 Stephanie Ascough
ISBN: 978-1-7349812-5-4

Published by Stephanie Ascough.
Editing by Cozy Cottage Editing.
Cover Art created by Stephanie Ascough.

For my sisters, who fix things they didn't break

TABLE OF CONTENTS

1. The Fey Graveyard

Our home was full of magic then. Not the strong, dangerous fey kind, of course; few humans interacted with them in our small town. Between Patience's gift with herbs and Charity's with flowers, the house always smelled of humble, kind, ordinary magic. My gift added nothing to our home's atmosphere. That was partly because the materials I work with have no fragrance. Also I rarely practiced it, and only then in secret, when the need was desperate.

My sisters and I sat in our small parlor as we awaited Father's return, talking of the small fortune we anticipated and arguing over whether to fix the roof first or buy new furniture. I was arranging intricate battle strategies on our worn, chipped Ward set, fighting a pretend opponent. Ward is chess's more complicated, aggressive cousin. My sisters were never interested in games like these.

"I know you are smart enough to learn," I said to Patience, for the fourth time this week. "Don't you want to set that herb weaving down for just half an hour and try something new?"

"Of course I'm smart enough. That doesn't work on me, Beauty. I know what I enjoy and I'm doing it now." Patience squinted at the intricate pattern in her lap. She never sounded more like the eldest than when she scolded me. "But it's time we decide where to move the furniture in the large parlor. When Father returns, we will get the roof fixed."

"So practical." Anyone else but us would have missed the faint sarcasm in Charity's low, musical voice. She was bent over a blanket she was embroidering for the miller's wife, who was expecting a baby. The firelight glimmered on delicate blue and red details. "Whatever would we do without two parlors?"

Patience put down her half-finished weaving and frowned at her. "There is no reason to let the whole roof rot in just because we don't use that room."

"And how much will that cost, Patience?" I asked, moving a piece into the enemy's side with a *click* against the board.

"I'm sure we will have enough. You know Father's never had a larger order for his wine, or from an establishment so well-known."

I bit the inside of my cheek. Patience would have rearranged the whole house if one of us mentioned a draft near our chair. But she did not keep our finances or know the true nature of our struggles. Of the three of us, I waited for Father's return with secret desperation, careful to never let it show.

"I wish I hadn't been silly enough to ask for a rose," mused Charity. She straightened up from her embroidery and stretched elegantly, like a cat. "I'm not sure it's late enough in the year for them yet."

"I don't regret asking him for more herbs," Patience declared. "That blasted blight took out all of my yarrow and most of the rosemary. Not a single kitchen garden in town escaped it, either. I need more of those if I'm to make my usual summer tinctures. Last year's store is almost gone. Whatever he brings me, I can propagate for anyone else who wishes to try growing it themselves."

"Why should you regret the rose, Charity?" I asked. "You have not asked for anything Father would begrudge you. And anyway, he's gone south where the weather is warmer."

"True." Charity shrugged, turning her large eyes to me. "Only it seems impractical when I have a garden full already."

"Nonsense. As the youngest, you must be spoiled. It's the rule," I said. "Isn't it, Patience?"

"Of course," she murmured around a sprig of herbs held fast between her teeth. Charity and I smiled at one another, knowing Patience had probably not heard us at all.

"And what about you, Beauty? Do you regret asking Father for a necklace?"

From anyone else, this would've been a veiled insult, one that I might have deserved. From my baby sister, it was merely a thoughtful inquiry. And I wished I could have answered her honestly. But to do so would have raised her and Patience's curiosity and therefore alarm.

I reached over and squeezed her knee. "No, Sweet. I don't regret asking for what I did."

I returned to my game and won against myself, but had lost all pleasure in it. My mind turned to money and to the necklace I had asked Father to bring me. It made me look greedy, and perhaps I was; but I would rather my sisters think me greedy than know what I really intended to do with my costly gift.

Father arrived just as we were setting our things aside for bed. We saw him ride up through the gate and dismount near the kitchen entrance. We ran downstairs, shouting and jostling like a bunch of children on baking day. I heard Clotilde, our cook, greet him, then scold him for bringing dirt inside. Something fluttered in my chest at his rejoinder. Even from behind the kitchen door he sounded subdued, sad, not his usual brisk self. It reminded me of how sunken he had seemed after Mother's death five years ago.

He came through the parlor door, his face bright and loving, and pulled us all into an embrace. Then, he kissed each of us on the head, from oldest to youngest. "My girls. *Pazi*, sit down, eh? *Bellezza*, still playing Ward? That's good. Ah, *Amore*. You all look the picture of health."

We smiled at his use of our names. When his eldest child was born he'd agreed to the name Patience, shortening it in his own language as an endearment, but he insisted on names for his other daughters that sounded pleasing in his estimation. He and our very French Mother had found their compromise. She hadn't minded that he used the more familiar word for love rather than charity for their youngest daughter.

"Come sit down, Father," said Charity, leading him to the fire and his favorite chair, while Patience called for Clotilde to bring them tea.

"I'm coming, Patience," said Clotilde, bustling in with a tray. She had been with us for many years. Gray-haired and sharp-eyed, she saw everything and usually spoke her mind. "Do you think I forgot? Try to live up to your name, girl." Her wry smile held affection, though, and Patience took the tray from her with an apologetic smile.

"Join us, won't you, Clotilde?"

"Tomorrow night, love," Clotilde replied, patting my sister's head. "Now that I've seen your father home and safe, I'm off to bed." And she went up to her room, returning our goodnight calls with a wave of the hand that pretended to be annoyed.

We were all settled when I asked, "How was it, *Papà*?"

I think my sisters saw something was wrong, now. Our father looked down at his cup, a line drawn sharp between his gray brows. "I am sorry to tell you, girls, that I could not bring what you asked for."

Patience and Charity rushed to reassure him that it didn't matter, but he patted Charity's hand with a sad smile.

"I'm afraid it does, for it is worse than you think. I received no payment for my wine because the wine never reached shore. I warned that captain against accepting fey cargo on board," he told us, his voice more weary than angry. "He refused to listen, the fool. And now, thanks to damned fey magic, everything sits at the bottom of the sea."

"Everything?" Patience echoed, but Father did not seem to hear her. Charity clasped Father's hand and murmured pity for the lost sailors. I stared at my rapidly cooling cup, my mind already darting a dozen steps ahead.

"You couldn't have done anything to stop it, Father," I said. "Let's drink our tea and go to bed. We all need the rest."

"Yes," Patience agreed. Really I meant that Father needed the rest, and she knew it. He had eaten little and would eat no more tonight. Charity stood with him, and when he looked at her his face cleared a little, and he spoke with more surety.

"We lost far too much on that ship, but we have something no fey magic can take from us," he said. "I don't want you to fret. None of you, do you understand me, *miei cari*?" He looked at each of us in turn, and I nodded along. "We will be well enough." He sounded sure, like his old self before Mother's death.

But I knew better. No payment and no necklace meant I had only one choice left.

Everyone else in the house was asleep when I crept from home, cloaked and silent as the night itself. No one needed to know where I was going. Grateful to be out of town and so near the woods, I hurried toward the whispering canopy and melted into the shadows.

A fey kingdom dwelt in these woods once, or so the story goes. Now there is nothing but a graveyard swathed in shadow and moss.

I had only been there once before. Despite the years between tonight and my last enterprise, I found my way easily when the clouds parted to reveal a waxing moon above. Anyone could find the trail leading in, but getting out would be difficult. After a few minutes' walk, I had to rely on landmarks: turn left at the lone, twisted oak, go past the fallen log now lost beneath a rippling blanket of fungi that glowed in the night. Fear and anticipation quickened my heartbeat.

The only jewelry I retained was a slim, gold ring my mother had left me, and I would never sell it. This left me with precious few options for raising income. Stories about the graveyard were as varied and contradictory as local gossip. It was said to be a place of forgotten treasures, if one could get past the spirits that haunted the place. Untold riches lay buried with their dead, left undisturbed by the wise and wary. Apparently I was neither. But I was desperate to test this particular tale. And I needed jewels in order to perform the magic my family preferred to ignore.

While we were all loving and loyal, this was the difference between my sisters and me: Patience and Charity would do anything to protect our family's feelings, but I would do anything to keep our family alive.

Despite the direness of our condition, my fingers itched with anticipation. I loved my magic as much as playing Ward. I hadn't felt this thrill in a long time.

When I stumbled into the clearing, the sight was just as jarring as I remembered.

The graves set at irregular intervals might have been hundreds or thousands of years old. Fey magic is said to preserve things for longer than is natural. At first glance the gravestones appeared to be tall monuments carved from great slabs of precious stones, or wrought from gold or silver in elaborate, delicate shapes. I had glimpsed them last time, along with what I hoped would be the fulfillment of my current search. But, like last time, when I moved into the clearing, these monuments writhed and blurred, contorting into shapes that sent a chill across my skin and caught the breath in my throat. They became bodies, twisted with age or torture, wild beasts of unfathomable savagery, and other things I did not recognize and had no wish to.

The chill was not just fear. The air was cold and clammy, still as death itself despite the frenzied, flickering movements before me. When I plunged ahead, it felt like wading through deep, turbid water, just as it had all those years ago.

A wave of dizziness forced me to still. Looking around and willing my racing heart to slow, I examined the shapes while attempting to emulate my eldest sister's patience. The gold and silver stones I ignored. Stumbling to the one closest to me, a rich, dark red like dried blood, I pulled a small garden shovel from my cloak and began to dig at the gravestone's base.

No angered spirit attacked me at the breaking of sacred soil. Nothing hindered me, save the palpable tug of the air around me. After a few minutes I found nothing in the earth and no hidden hollow in the stone itself. After searching several gravestones, my path winding through a forest of corpses and other horrors, frustration and panic started to build in my throat. If I found nothing, then what?

I dragged myself to one stone that, when not an image of horror, looked like a dark red stone similar to the first, clear as claret and crimson as rage. When I reached it, something odd happened.

It ceased changing, allowing me a closer look while the other stones continued their macabre dance. Like most, it was taller than I, etched with faded words in a strange language. Dropping to my knees, I struck the earth.

Clink. Something lay glittering, half-covered in the dirt. I scrabbled and scraped until, with sweating, shaking hands, I pulled up a slender rope that caught the weak strands of moonlight and glimmered with promise.

Clods of dirt fell away as I lifted my find for closer inspection. It was cool, jointed, hard as greed. Still no deathly attack fell upon me, and still I breathed, and the object in my hand filled me with raw, ragged joy.

It was a necklace fit for a queen. A fey queen, more like. An intricate gold chain cupped five radiant crimson stones, the color of the gravestone. The middle one was the largest, the size of a grape and round as a coin.

Rubies were the rarest of stones in the human world. I had asked Father for a lone sapphire in a setting of silver, or at best an emerald, knowing I could trade two stones for one of greater value until I had enough. But surely this alone would pay our debts. I pocketed my findings and turned to leave when everything went dark as the inside of a well in midwinter.

Too late.

Now my limbs felt weightless, limp, like those of a marionette with its strings cut. The image of a man cloaked in shadows flashed before my eyes, and a voice like the whispering of a hundred withered wings breathed in my ear.

2. The Visitor

You are bold, human.

I could not speak. My limbs remained unresponsive, and all I knew was the terror of being held at the mercy of an unseen power.

I see how much you want this. Your greed is strong and startling. I have not seen its like in many, many years.

My heart in my throat, I clutched the necklace in my pocket, as if by my will alone I could keep what I had stolen.

What to do with you, troublemaker? The voice ebbed and flowed, yet I could have sworn there was a playful, almost careless edge to it. *I cannot let you go without leaving something in return. This graveyard demands a price. You must understand that. So what shall it be?*

I struggled to speak. A number of things I might offer came to mind, but I doubted any of them would suffice.

Yes, it is difficult, even when you have the gift of choosing your own sacrifice. And there is no returning what you have stolen. You cannot avoid the cost. Well, then. I remove the burden of choice from you.

Suddenly I could feel my hands attached to my limbs, the strain in my back as I tried to extricate myself from this unseen guardian of the graveyard. My feet stood on solid ground.

I will choose your sacrifice.

The voice was little more than the sighing of the wind, and as the last word faded, my eyes cleared and the graveyard swam into view. I gasped for air, struggling to stay upright. The necklace remained in my hand. It was cold as ice.

As I ran home through the moon-limned forest, the last words haunted me like the spirit who had spoken them. What would it choose, and how would I know? Would I lose my voice, my mind, my looks? I might lose my magic—that thought troubled me greatly and spurred me on. Without my magic, I could not save my family from ruin. The thought sparked hot anger inside me.

I thought of my Ward game, simple and clumsy. I would have gladly relinquished it as protection against such a force with unknown powers. But I doubted a fey spirit, or whatever kind of spirit that was, would find such a gift an acceptable trade.

Yet I did not pause in my flight. Whatever the cost might be, I would happily pay it if it meant my family's salvation.

Not far from the forest's edge I stumbled into a shock of cold water. I had forgotten the stream in my haste, but it gave me an idea. I splashed myself until I was soaked through and gasping, uncomfortable but awake and hoping that I had washed the scent of fey magic away.

Perhaps the spirit only made empty threats, I thought as I broke through the forest. The fey were known to toy carelessly with humans from time to time. I had not ventured that far into the graveyard last time, nor encountered any spirits then, either. The spirit seemed tied to the place. Surely it still was, along with its power? I took my escape as proof of this, determining to do anything in my power to avoid losing to this capricious force.

I pushed these thoughts from my mind as I entered the house through the kitchen and crept upstairs, avoiding the creaking steps, my mind set on a singular task.

After changing quickly, I set the necklace in a pool of candlelight, the rubies glimmering like liquid fire. My fingers tingled as I shut my eyes and pictured the first stone, the size of my thumbnail, stretching and breaking into two identical ones. The magic, called double alchemy because it could create two jewels out of one, pulled through my fingers, and my breathing began to struggle; sweat dampened my skin. I knew this feeling well, knew how to endure and to continue on.

But something pushed against me, sudden and powerful. My head swam and I stifled the scream rising in my throat as the ground seemed to spin me upside down. This had never happened before. I forced down my nausea, holding on to the object of my magic, straining until I thought I would break.

Plink.

I opened my eyes and sucked in a breath, gasping as my swirling senses returned to my body's upright position. My clothes stuck to my back with sweat the way nausea clung to my throat. The strange force remained, but it was weaker, receding, then gone.

A perfect copy of the first stone lay next to the necklace, rocking slightly.

Done.

A fierce sense of accomplishment drew from me a tired smile. The aftereffects then hit me, and I slumped forward. Double alchemy is exhausting, but this fatigue was unusually severe. I fought to keep my eyes open long enough to put the jewels somewhere safe and crawled into bed. I barely had energy to wonder about the strange resistance, different from anything I had ever encountered while performing double alchemy. Could it be cursed?

Anything from that graveyard could be. But whatever the cause of the resistance, it had not stopped me from achieving my purpose.

Tomorrow, I would begin on the next one. I would reproduce all five gems to sell and bring in enough money to pay our debts.

So far, my plan was succeeding.

But I had underestimated the resistance housed within those precious gems.

I was hardly out of bed the next morning when Clotilde knocked on my door.

"What is it?" I asked when I stumbled to my door. Her eyes were wide, her face pale. Instant fear seized me. "Is it Father? Or—"

"No, Beauty, they're all still abed." She cut me off with a wave of her hand. "But there's a—a strange gentleman downstairs, and—well, he's demanding to see you. I would say you must come down at once, but—"

Fear marked her face. She clutched her shawl and looked down the stairs, as if expecting to see someone following her. I patted her hand.

"It's all right, Clotilde." It most certainly was not. I feared the creditors had already arrived. Well, it was best that I meet them myself. Father would be weary from his journey, and my dear, foolish sisters had no head for money between them.

"He's *magical*, Beauty."

Ah. No wonder she didn't want to wake Father. But when had he ever had dealings with the fey? For that must be who Clotilde referred to, as Father had no qualms about my sisters' magic or most other human magic skill. I dearly wished he were as understanding toward double alchemy.

20

Instead he believed magic like mine was too similar to fey magic.

"Right," I said. "Never mind my clothes, Clotilde. He'll be gone before the rest of the house stirs." I gritted my teeth at the thought of anyone coming to make trouble. Adjusting my dressing robe and my braid, I straightened and descended the steps, following the good woman to our large parlor. Clotilde fled back upstairs.

I squared my shoulders and entered the room.

I had never seen the fey before. Tales abound of their cruelty, their cunning, and their beauty. Clotilde had told us many. I had imagined some coldly elegant being, but even my imagination had not prepared me for a face-to-face encounter.

The fey man before me was unusually tall. He had pale skin, high cheekbones, and dark blond hair cut just above broad shoulders. His ears were slightly pointed, and the severe frown upon his face did nothing to mar his unearthly, intimidating grace.

But he was in our house, uninvited. I decided he was nothing more than an unusually good-looking person with terrible manners and returned his stare with all the pride I could muster. "How can I be of service?"

"You can return what you have stolen at once." His voice was musical and deep.

"I beg your pardon?" I stuttered. Of all things to be accused of, theft was not on my list.

"I believe I spoke clearly."

"You have just accused me of thieving," I replied. "I demand to know who lays these charges at my feet."

"The court of Clear Star." Somehow he drew himself up even taller.

The name of Clear Star belonged to no town or city I knew, but if he would not be more forthcoming, neither would I. "I don't know what you are talking about."

21

"Yes, you do." The strange visitor stepped closer to me, eyes gleaming, and I resisted the urge to step back. "There is no mistaking the necklace in your possession."

"And how is that?" I replied, as much from a desire to stall him as from genuine curiosity. "I have said nothing about a necklace. I would like to know how you reached such a ridiculous conclusion."

His eyes narrowed and his voice sharpened. "I will do no such thing. Bring it at once."

"No." I steeled myself beneath his unnerving stare. "You disturb my household and demand something that I don't have and for which you can offer me no proof of ownership. You may leave."

"The magic does not lie any better than you do." My strange guest considered me for a moment. "And I would rather not kill you."

"Oh." I had not missed the sword at his side. Considering my options, I began to see that it might be best to go along with his demand. My magic was no match for the fey. Clearly, I had to get him out of the house as quickly as possible. And my mind spun with ideas: I may yet be able to work this situation to my own advantage.

"Very well." I gestured toward one of the brocaded silk couches in the parlor, the one directly under a poorly patched leak. Water stains spread across the once-rich, pale pink fabric. "I will return with the necklace at once." Leaving him to make himself comfortable, I went to retrieve it, furiously spinning a plan along the way.

I returned a few moments later, relieved, at least, that no one else was awake. I held the small satin bag carrying my stolen treasure. The fey, who had not seated himself, reached to take it.

"Tell me something," I said, snatching it back just out of reach. "I encountered a strange resistance while reproducing one of the stones. You are familiar with double alchemy, a kind of human magic?"

A muscle jumped in his jaw. He remained silent, and I continued, "I have performed double alchemy enough to know that this resistance isn't ordinary. I would even hazard to guess that there is a curse on this necklace, and it is a fey curse, or I am a newborn baby. My double alchemy could weaken this curse."

He grunted. "There is no guarantee of that."

So it *was* cursed, and I had found an opening in this person's resistance. "But there is a chance! You admitted as much."

"What do you want?" His voice was strong and even as ever, but his impressive scowl flickered with doubt. I suspected he was not the one ruling Clear Star, but an emissary, and he could bring me to the one in charge. I pressed my suit.

"If you must take this necklace, let me go too, and meet whoever demands its return."

A cold laugh escaped his lips. "You ask too much for a human." He folded his arms and paced, giving me one sidelong glance. "Very well. You have five minutes."

He was muttering regrets under his breath when I flew from the room and up the stairs as if the fey himself followed me, but this time with a thrill of triumph.

"Beauty! What are you doing?"

I jolted to a stop when Patience's voice hissed at me. She stood in front of Clotilde on the stair landing above me, glaring down with a mixture of anger and fear. Clotilde shook her head as if to indicate she had tried and failed to keep my sister away.

"I have no time to explain," I whispered. I could hear Father's footsteps creaking in his bedchamber. "It is a matter of our livelihood, Patience."

"But I smell strange magic on you." Her nose wrinkled with distaste. "All heaven's stars help you, Beauty, if Father finds out. And when you come back, he will. You won't be able to rid yourself of it."

I paused, thinking. "Can you help me? Brew some kind of potion to disguise or remove the smell of fey magic?"

Too late, I realized I had said the wrong thing. Anxious triumph lit Patience's face. She had only been guessing at the kind of visitor waiting downstairs. Unlike Clotilde, she had had no direct encounter with the fey before.

"I knew it! Oh, how could you, Beauty? What are you thinking?"

"Please, Patience. I have no other choice. I am doing this to spare *Papà*. I would have spared you, too, if you hadn't been so nosy."

Patience bit her lip, and her brows gathered like a storm cloud. "Come home through the kitchen and I'll see to the brew," she said.

"Thank you."

Patience shrank against the wall, forcing Clotilde to sidestep her. "Don't touch me! I don't want to smell like *that*."

I blew her a kiss instead and hurried up. Moments later I went outside to find a stately carriage before our house, and the fey man holding open the door for me. The whole carriage was painted deep blue, and four black horses, normal looking enough though tall and very fine, stamped and snorted at the front. There was no sign of footmen or a driver. I entered without comment.

The seats were deep and comfortable. My reluctant companion gave me another cold stare; in the dark interior, his eyes caught a shard of outside light and glowed.

The carriage took us in the opposite direction from town, veered from the road, and entered the forest. I could see no track ahead. Our destination must lie very far away if we were in search of fey land. But then, what else had I expected?

"Is it true, that fey do not care for humans?"

My companion merely straightened his coat and continued gazing out the window.

The carriage had rolled smoothly along, but now the sound changed. Heedless of propriety, I stuck my head out the window and gasped.

The forest stood a respectful distance from us on either side. How we had entered the woods without so much as a scratch upon the carriage was a question I didn't care to contemplate, and besides, the sight before me commanded all my attention. We rode on a fine gravel road that ended in a spired monstrosity nearly the size of a small village. By comparison, our house was a hovel. And that, I reminded myself, is where we would end up if my plan failed.

I sat back in the carriage and let the sight swirl before my mind's eye, where I could look it over in private. I had heard the fey had royalty and paupers and everything in between. Whoever lived here was certainly more akin to the first.

When I followed my silent companion from the carriage, I could only gawk like the human commoner I was.

Magic overflowed in this place, of this there was no doubt. Lush rose bushes graced the drive, their fragrance intermingling with the ever-stronger scent of fey power. I thought how Charity would marvel at them as only she could. Pristine gravel paths laced their way throughout vast gardens, indicating an immense property. I hoped that Patience had a strong enough brew to wash away the lingering smell when I was done, for I was surely steeped in it by now.

"I suggest we don't keep him waiting," the fey man said, drawing my attention away from the lavish surroundings.

The castle doorway was so wide and so tall that three carriages could have passed through side by side. I glimpsed elaborate towers, windows at least two stories tall, and massive gray stone walls before the man led me through a small side door. We went through a series of narrow hallways and tightly winding stone staircases, and though I've always had a strong sense of direction, the experience was completely disorienting. Just as I began to wonder if this was all just a fey trap leading to my demise, the fey man stopped before a plain little door and ushered me inside.

It was a small, dim chamber, where the light of a single candle brushed velvet curtains drawn against the day, and two tall, stately brocaded chairs facing each other, one with its back to me. The candle seemed to hover between them. Hints of other shapes stood bathed in shadow.

"Tristan," said a male voice from somewhere in the room, low and threatening, "who have you brought to me?"

3. A Game of Chance

I could see no one. My mind began to whirl as fingers of panic reached to grip me, but I was no stranger to keeping calm in the face of the unknown. I had anticipated some grand, bright throne room meant to intimidate me into compliancy, but this place felt heavy with fey magic in a way that a concentrated herbal tonic might assault the senses. The last thing I wished to do was to give this unseen challenger any hint that he had the upper hand—even though, as I was in a fey castle, this was undoubtedly true.

"A thief, my lord," Tristan answered from behind me. "She found the necklace."

"And why," continued the unseen interrogator, "did you think it necessary to bring her along?"

"You may wish to hear what she has to say," replied Tristan evenly.

"I have no time for troublesome humans. Send her away at once, and put a forgetting spell on her. We do not need her poking her nose about here in search of fey treasure."

"Nevertheless, my lord. She may prove useful."

I heard a slow, angry exhale. "Did I not make myself clear?"

His tone was dangerously low, every word measured. I was mildly surprised when Tristan answered in the same calm voice as before.

"As starlight, my lord," he said. "All the same. It relates to our current situation."

"You dare speak of this now?"

The silence that followed laced the air with a deadly tension, like poison waiting to take effect. But my panic had receded into something familiar. I was ready to speak for myself. This was the thrill of a challenge, and I would not leave without putting forward my planned proposal.

"Wait," I interjected. Stepping further into the room, I tried to seek out this person in the shadows. Still, I saw no living being. Was he, too, some disembodied spirit? Perhaps even the spirit I had encountered in the graveyard? Their voices were different, but then again, such a difference was likely easy to achieve for a fey who could choose invisibility. "I understand a curse resides in this necklace. I may be able to weaken it."

Harsh laughter sounded. "You? How?"

I told him of the resistance I had encountered in my practice of double alchemy. All the while, I silently pleaded for my suspicion to be true, that the fey Tristan would not have agreed to bring me along if there were no chance of my skills being useful. Silence greeted me when I finished my speech.

"Leave us, Tristan."

The door shut behind me with a click, and I was alone with a person I couldn't see. Tristan's departure left me with a bizarre wish for his return. Better the fey you can see, I thought.

A low, brief chuckle startled me. "You harass my councilman into bringing you here and spin this outrageous tale of double alchemy. I must say I admire your boldness."

"I did not come here to be admired. And I speak the truth—my lord," I added, as an afterthought.

"Well. No need to stand on ceremony. Please, sit." His voice was brisk, almost cordial, but I continued my search as I approached the two chairs by the fireplace. Maybe he sat in the one facing me.

Both were empty. I chose one to lower myself into, and—

"Pleasant as the thought may be, I hardly think our first meeting calls for you to sit on my lap," said the voice from behind me.

I whirled, sat down in the opposite chair with stiff grace, and glared.

A flash of white appeared—a grin or an eye, I wasn't sure, but it was gone a moment later, lost to the candlelight-touched darkness shrouding the chair. At least now I knew where he was—I hoped. Something else caught my eye. The candle on the table was not alone.

Catching the light in every tiny point and polished surface sat the most beautiful Ward game I could have imagined. How had I missed it before? The material was hard to identify—crystal, maybe, or emeralds for all I could tell—but this was no crude wooden set. Its worth was at least equal to the necklace in my hands. My original plan morphed and grew like a mushroom after a rainy spell.

"Show me the necklace."

I retrieved the necklace and the duplicated stone, holding them out. "You see? Notice these two gems are identical. My skill in double alchemy produced the duplicate, as I said."

I waited for a hand to appear, for him to demand I relinquish the treasure.

"Double alchemy is rare," he mused. "Even among humans. Even fey do not possess the gift."

I gestured with the necklace. "I could demonstrate now, if you do not believe me."

"That is unnecessary and unsafe without a full understanding the nature of this necklace. But this is fascinating. You worm your way into a fey castle, demanding to meet me; and though I sense your fear, you do your best not to show it. I think purloining a necklace is a small thing for you, compared to your other abilities and desires. I think that beneath your unassuming appearance, you are made of fire and steel."

This turn of conversation surprised me so much that I could not find a reply. While his voice had been harsh and cold when I'd first heard him speak, it had softened during our exchange. It was not as formidable as Tristan's was when he had arrived at my home. Yet it gave me the uncanny feeling of being seen in a way no one had seen me before.

I cleared my throat. "Forgive me, my lord, but you did not invite me to sit for a chat."

"Alas, no. To business, then: What do you want? A reward? A spell? I suppose you want money."

"I want an answer to my question first. How do I know this necklace is truly yours?"

"Do you frequent fey lands and courts? Often have fey appear at your home?"

"No."

"Then I suppose you must take my word for it."

"I found it in a fey graveyard. How would you know about it, if it belonged to the dead?"

"I never knew humans could be so impertinent," he murmured to himself. "I've no idea how it came to be in a graveyard. That is a matter for further investigation. But I doubt you would understand our fey means of learning and discovery, and I cannot leave this castle. Why should I gallivant in graveyards? Now, tell me. What do you truly want?"

"I said earlier that I believe my magic weakened the spell. Is that possible?"

He drew in a breath. "Possible, yes. Likely, no."

"If you allow me to finish my work, to copy each stone for myself, then you could have your necklace back, and you will know how much I have weakened this curse for you."

"No." The answer came swiftly, decisively. The shadow shook as if a hand waved away some impossible thought. "You have already tampered with something you do not understand. I reject your conditions. Return it at once."

"I can't believe you'd want this necklace just for its aesthetic qualities."

"Humans have no place in solving fey problems." There was a note of something in his voice now, something that suggested I had hit close to a nerve.

I settled back in my chair. "Do you have other means?"

"My means and my reasons are not your concern. Return it. I won't tell you again."

"I propose a wager instead." I tried to hide my eagerness by gesturing toward the Ward game. "Do you play, my lord?"

A silence followed. I prayed he wasn't about to oust me magically from the room for my impudence, or worse.

"You have been staring at that game with the hunger of a starving man," he said, and I could have sworn he was smiling. I wished again that the light would reveal something, anything of this man. When he chuckled, he sounded almost triumphant, as if the tables had turned in his favor. "Fire and steel."

"If you win, I leave the necklace and never trouble you again," I pressed. "If I win, you agree to my terms."

"Your terms." He seemed resistant but uncertain. "As much as I admire your stubbornness, the fact remains: none of this concerns you."

"But it does." I was used to being underestimated by men, but I was not used to interacting with one who presented such tantalizing challenge, and invisible or not, my questioner had revealed something important. He did

31

not want my help, yet he felt conflicted. I could use that to my advantage. Whether he truly admired my stubbornness or simply found me amusing didn't matter.

"I am trying to save my family," I went on, my sincerity no act. "If I don't pay the bank in time, we will lose our home and most of our possessions. This necklace is my last chance."

I lowered my eyes to the blood-red gems in my lap. Once again I felt exposed, but at least this time I had chosen it. The presence across from me remained silent for so long I began to wonder if he had melted into thin air and become a true shadow.

"This curse is far beyond you," he said, not dismissively.

"Yet despite encountering resistance, I have successfully reproduced one stone. It yields to me somehow. Surely it would benefit us both to find out just how much I can make it yield. Here." I held the necklace out. "See for yourself, milord."

I watched for a hand, a shadow, a claw, anything to reach out and take the necklace, but nothing did. "Tell me the rest of your terms," he said.

"I will duplicate the rest of these rubies before I leave the original with you for good. And one more thing. For every winning move, the loser must answer a question of the opponent's choice."

"Agreed. But I add my own condition: if you win, you must perform your double alchemy here."

This was ideal. I could leave the necklace here and avoid bringing any whiff of fey magic home, provided Patience could brew a suitable potion to wash it from me. It only now occurred to me that I would have had trouble keeping the scent contained to my room if I'd kept it there.

"Done," I said, struggling to hide my elation. I laid the necklace over the arm of my chair, its facets catching just the faintest shards of light. "Will you begin, my lord?"

This was not just politeness. I still wanted to see his hand move a game piece, anything to let me catch a glimpse of the person who seemed so full of opposites.

"Your move."

I glanced at the board to find he had set his first piece ahead. Somehow I'd missed it. I calculated and took my position, determined to keep my eyes on the game. Yet after a few more minutes, I still had not seen him move at all. At least I claimed my first triumph when I seized the first piece.

"You owe me an answer, my lord."

"Go on."

"What is your name?"

"You may call me Armand," he said, his voice schooled to neutrality.

"What about your title? Surely in a place like this—"

"I believe I answered your question. My title is of no concern when games are played between equals. Ah." Yet again, he moved a piece without me seeing, claiming one of mine. "And what is your name? It is only fair."

I sighed. He was a worthy opponent, and his question was fair, but I didn't like answering it. "My name is Beauty."

"Not an ill-fitting name at all. Yet you are unhappy with it."

"It comes with certain expectations, and they do not normally include intelligence."

"That hardly seems fair."

"It isn't," I said, surprised by his sincerity. "When people hear 'beauty,' they think of delicate grace and a preference for only the visually pleasing, and I hate to be taken simply as an ornament when I have a mind for numbers and for challenges, for—"

I broke off abruptly. *Scheming and bold plans* died on my tongue, the vehemence of my own words catching me off guard.

"You hate to be underestimated," Armand said quietly. "I think anyone would be a fool to underestimate you."

I bit my tongue.

We went back and forth for a while in this fashion, and still I never saw him move. It was as if something shifted my gaze so that I would think I was looking in the right place, only to find a piece had shifted on the board.

Still, we each won a few more questions. Was he a prince? He said yes, but refused any formal address. That explained the grandeur. He asked me to describe the graveyard, which I did briefly, not mentioning the spirit. He had never heard of it. With my next victory, I wanted to know what kind of spell was attached to the necklace.

"I begin to regret agreeing to this game," Armand mused. "All you need to know at present is that the curse removed this whole estate and all who live here from our country, depositing us in the forest without means to return."

This inspired a dozen more questions, but I kept them for later. We went back and forth again, and the game grew tense.

"Where did you learn to play this game?" Armand asked after claiming another piece of mine.

This felt uncomfortable, but I wouldn't let him know it. I eyed the game board as I answered. "I learned when I was a girl. The girls' school and the boys' school were next to each other, and I was fascinated with the game, which the boys played during the lunch hour. I caught on faster than they did. As the year went by, I played and beat every one of them. They told me I could join their club if I—if I did something they dared me to do. And even though I succeeded, they changed their minds." I stretched my arms out and tapped the table absentmindedly. "They are now an elite men's club. They compete in other towns and win a good deal of money, I hear. And no one in our town will play Ward because it is considered too exclusive, and now my sisters, who didn't care about it before, can't be bothered to touch it with a broom handle."

"That's quite a tale."

Armand's voice surprised me. Again there was no hint of mockery or teasing in his words. He sounded utterly sincere, and that made me realize once again just how much I had shared without intending to. "There is far more to you than beauty," he said. "I understand the fire and steel, I think."

"Just because we're playing Ward," I said, "does not mean you know me at all." I moved my highest-ranking piece to claim his, smiling with undisguised triumph. "I have won the game. My final question is this: What do you look like? I would like to see your face."

"I think not," came the reply.

"Why not? It is a fair question. More than fair, when you have seen me this whole time and I have not even seen your hand play once across the board." I leaned closer, trying to pierce the shadows where my adversary sat. "You cannot cheat when we have both established the precedent of following the rules."

"I could simply describe myself."

I shook my head. "You know that won't do. How would I know you weren't making yourself out to be more handsome than you are?"

Armand chuckled. "And if I refuse?"

"It would make you a poor player and a cheat, milord."

He chuckled again, a smooth, satisfied sound. "A thief and a cheat? We would make a wicked pair."

I folded my hands in my lap and waited.

"Very well. I will keep my honor for you, thief," he said at last, "though in truth I'd rather continue this game. But since you have bested me . . ." Slowly, the shadow unfolded from the chair.

At first I could make nothing out, other than that the prince was very tall, and broad-shouldered, too. Then for an instant the candlelight gilded his face.

He had none.

Whatever I had taken for teeth or eyes was gone now. It was as if a thick veil covered his features from head to foot, though none were visible and he had made no move to cover himself. The light simply slid over his face without finding purchase and settled on a more receptive surface elsewhere. He looked like a shadow made substantial.

"Well, Beauty," said Armand, "am I a cheater still?"

"I do not know what you are, my lord," I said, "except a fey prince who plays Ward well."

The shadow folded back into his chair and melted into the layers of darkness. "And I might tell you more," he said, "but our game is ended."

"And our deal?" I pressed. "Will you honor my terms or not?"

"Return tomorrow, if it suits. We will see if your double alchemy can, in fact, weaken the curse." There was a faint sound of distant bells. "Leave the necklace with me. I will see what I can learn of it."

The door opened and the councilman entered. "Tristan," Armand demanded, "take our guest home at once. She will return tomorrow at the same time. Who knows, we may yet find another game with which to amuse ourselves."

With his orders to Tristan, the brusque harshness had reentered his voice, but Armand had addressed the last sentence to me in a softer tone. I stood, curtsied, and turned to go when the fey prince spoke again.

"One more thing. I swear a binding oath to fulfill my end of the agreement. No harm shall come to you under this roof."

The words held a weight that surprised me. Looking at his shadow from the door, I nodded slowly and formed what I hoped was a suitable reply. "I swear I will hold to my side of the agreement."

The words seemed to satisfy Armand, for he offered no correction. Before the door closed, I glimpsed back at the great, shadowed chair and almost thought it held nothing at all.

Tristan did not look amused at my request, but he stopped the carriage some distance from the house and held the door open for me to descend. "Be ready tomorrow," he said in a grim voice, and soon he and the carriage had disappeared back into the forest.

My walk gave me more time than I would have liked to think about my encounter with Armand. The uncanny feeling of being seen in a way that my closest friends—my sisters—did not, by a stranger shrouded in mystery, persisted no matter how swiftly I walked. I tried to push it away when our house came into view.

I entered through the garden gate. The perfume of roses filled the air, rich and salty-sweet. Charity's ever-expanding assortment always bloomed early. I hoped it would cover the smell of magic clinging to me like smoke, especially since I hadn't doused myself in the stream this time, and was relieved that my youngest sister wasn't there to ask me questions. Opening the kitchen door, I gasped in shock as a shower of cold water doused me from above.

Patience's light laughter floated out. Flinging back my strong-smelling hair, I could see a small bucket swinging wildly from a slim cord. The other end of the cord was fastened to a sturdy kitchen chair. Patience had always lived up to her name in the way that a viper waits for its prey: watchful and precise. She smiled sweetly at my glare.

"Is it strong enough for you, dearest?" she asked, drying a dish.

"You might have warned me," I sputtered.

"I might have."

At least the telltale signs of magic were gone; instead I smelled as if I'd rolled in Patience's herb garden. "Do either of them suspect?"

Patience's wry smile turned serious as she handed me a towel. "No. And Father is still in town, looking for work." She squinted, scrutinizing me uncomfortably. "You're going back there, aren't you? How many times am I going to have to make this?"

I thought about lying or giving her a specific number to placate her, but that wasn't fair. "I don't know," I confessed. "Not too long, I should think. But I have made a bargain that will answer our financial difficulties, Patience. It will be worth it."

Her eyes widened. "You made a *bargain* with the fey?" She looked equal parts shocked, dismayed, and uncertain, and she grabbed my arm so hard that her nails dug into my skin through the fabric. "Beauty, what in all the worlds were you thinking? How could you do this to *Papà*? To *yourself*?"

I yanked my arm away. "You don't understand our financial situation. We are bankrupt, Patience. Yes, Father said the loss of his shipment was not the end, but Father does not know the extent of it, either. Tristan won't be the only unwanted visitor soon. We shall have to sell everything—everything—to live. We will lose our home if I don't do this. How else will we survive? Do *you* have a plan?"

I drew in a shaking breath. Guilt for speaking to Patience in such a way filled me, yet it didn't eclipse the bitter relief I felt at sharing this burden. I'd carried it for too long. Maybe speaking so boldly with the prince earlier had loosened something within me, some old stone dislodged and sent hurtling down a hill.

"All right." Her voice was little more than a whisper. She set her mouth in a thin line and swiftly tugged the bucket free from its cord. "You don't have to tell me what you're doing. I know better than to argue with you. Now get dressed before Father returns. And for the sake of us all, Beauty"—she bit her lip in worry—"stay as safe as you can."

I nodded and went inside, feeling sheepish yet convinced there was no use in talking anymore about the matter.

4. In the Dark

No one else at home suspected a thing. We ate dinner as usual, then read together in the small parlor and persuaded Clotilde to join us. I looked around at the familiar surroundings: the picture of Mother, gentle and smiling over the mantlepiece, whose white moldings needed a good cleaning and fresh paint; the large, threadbare settee where Charity and Clotilde sat, Father's red-cushioned chair that had faded almost to brown, and the matching chair that Patience and I tried to force one another into using. We both refused to give in, and so sat on the scrubbed stone floor. Even Laurine, Patience's love and the town's new blacksmith, came by, entering into our banter with the ease of familiarity.

Clinging to our usual rhythms was both comforting and frustrating, an anchor and a farce. I glanced at the Ward game in the corner. It looked very crude compared to the one I had wielded today. And I felt a thrill at the thought of going back to the fey estate and in meeting a mind who saw things clearly as I did, if perhaps a little too clearly for comfort.

Tristan arrived at the same time next morning. I was prepared, waiting on the kitchen doorstep where I had a better view of the forest than from the front door. The scent of herbs and roses stirred in a gentle morning breeze, not yet full of summer's heat. I was at the carriage door before Tristan opened it and met his glare with a bright smile.

"I hope, though I doubt, that you grasp the weight of this," he said when we'd been riding for some time. "Do you begin to understand how much rests on your actions?"

"I believe I do," I said, surprised. Of course I didn't understand the full extent for him and Armand and the whole kingdom, and I kept from pointing out that he had been less than forthcoming. And I noted that while he and Armand both spoke with sharpness, Armand's was directed at Tristan and held an open, unforgiving rebuke, while Tristan's tone seemed to be an earnestness congruent with his nature.

"This castle isn't where it belongs. If you interfere with the curse in any negative way, I will have you out before you can blink."

I pushed a dozen other questions away. "Why should I interfere negatively? The only way I know how to meddle with fey magic is through my own. My family's survival depends on this partnership. I made no promises I cannot keep. You and your prince have the power here, not I, and we both know this."

I didn't stop a hint of indignation from hardening my voice, and Tristan seemed to consider my speech.

"We are all waiting to be reunited with more than one person we love." Something odd—grief?—flickered briefly in his eyes, surprising me, but his voice remained hard and I knew better than to push for further details.

Tristan led me through the small side door, but instead of upstairs, the grim fey led me so far down the same spiral staircase that, once again, candles served as our only light. I would not betray my growing apprehension by asking a question. But when he stopped at a door bound by a strange metal and opened it into utter darkness, I hesitated.

"He is waiting," Tristan said.

"Here?" I asked, my curiosity getting the better of me. "You'll see."

They had no cause to harm me, if there was a chance I, a mere mortal, could break a powerful fey curse. I followed Tristan into the gloom, hearing our footsteps echo in what must be a vast cavern of a room. I could just make out Tristan's head, but everything else was shrouded in utter darkness.

"I will return soon. You have nothing to fear," said Tristan, and then he was gone, his footsteps growing fainter and fainter up the stairs. I was alone.

And angry. How long would I wait here? Why was it so important I remain in a place that reminded me of a dungeon? Was this, after all, some kind of terrible joke? I promised myself I would extract more details from either councilman or prince as soon as I could.

"I suppose His Royal Highness is too busy to bother himself with me today," I groused aloud.

"His Royal Highness is never too busy for charming guests."

I gave a frightened yelp when Armand spoke somewhere nearby, which only made me angrier. "How long have you been lurking?"

"Beauty," he said pleasantly. "I am glad you've returned. I only just arrived."

I snorted, noting the amusement in his voice as I scrounged for some decorum.

I found only a little.

"Why here, my lord?" I asked, repeating my question from earlier. "The dark may give you an advantage, but it does the opposite for me."

"I shall have to be more specific with my instructions to Tristan in the future," he murmured. Footsteps approached. "My room is currently unsuitable. But more

42

importantly, you were at a disadvantage in our last meeting. I can remedy that here."

The footsteps drew nearer. A faint form emerged from the darkness. I squinted in an imitation of Patience—then I saw him.

Before me stood the complete image of a man like a reflection in a dusty old mirror. I could just make out light skin, smooth, light brown hair, and broad shoulders. He was tall, as the fey seemed to be. I glimpsed piercing brown eyes, a long nose, an expressive mouth, and a firm chin. Then he was gone. His features disappeared, leaving the image of his face nothing more than a vague outline before me and a distinct impression in my mind.

"I am only visible in the dark," he said.

I stared mutely, remembering the eyes that spoke volumes. I had seen an intensity about them that hinted at much more behind his self-contained manner from yesterday. It made me wonder what other secrets he held.

"You were," I replied. "But now I can't see you."

"Well. Visible now and then." Humor touched his voice. "Does it help you feel more at ease?"

"I was perfectly at ease last time," I lied. Although given the startling quality of his beauty, I felt even more flustered this time than I had at our first meeting, and struggled even more to hide my discomfort.

Trying to change my train of thought, I asked, "Does it feel odd, being invisible?"

"No." He sounded as though he didn't expect my question but found it amusing. "But I don't enjoy being unable to see myself. And the council members are losing patience with me as I took them from their families. It is my fault we are here."

Since he had answered my impudent question without a pause, I went on. "Yes, about that, my lord. I would like to know more about the curse."

The vague head nodded, and even in his diaphanous state, he gave the impression of dignity and an impressive physical bearing. "I haven't much to tell you. We have seen the effects of the curse, experienced many ourselves, guessed what others might be when the corridors grow strange and confusing and certain rooms disappear. All night I spent examining the necklace, but have only confirmed that she cast a complicated spell. She was very powerful."

"She?" I prompted, hesitantly.

When he answered, I noted how different he sounded: grieved, upset. "A dear friend of mine. She felt injured that I . . . did not feel for her as she did for me. She cast this place and everyone in it from the kingdom. We are stranded in the forest, cut off from the country of Clear Star with no way of returning unless the curse breaks. I have never had the strength of magic she did."

That explained *why*. "I wondered if the curse had turned you to—" I began, floundering in my own awkward question, but Armand intercepted.

"By the gods, you don't hold back, do you? You want to know if I have always been like this." A shadowed arm waved, a gesture of both acknowledgment and futility. "No, I have not. I'll tell you my belief. It is a punishment for my vanity. My curse-caster may have thought I loved myself too much."

"Do you?"

The prince chuckled. "I was incredibly vain, yes. But there, at least, I believe I have changed."

The image of his face, especially his eyes, lingered in my mind. Small wonder he had thought so well of himself. And yet when I had seen him, there had been no hint of self-importance.

"You found the necklace in a fey graveyard," Prince Armand prompted.

"Yes," I answered, recalled to the present. "It's said to be full of treasures. I only needed one." Though how a necklace belonging to him found its way there, I still couldn't guess. As he seemed much more forthcoming today, I had more pressing questions. "How *did* you find me, if no one has entered the human world before?"

"Two nights ago the entire castle flickered like a candle, indicating something or someone had interfered with our condition. Tristan followed the newly turned up magic to you. The necklace was a gift from me, but she used it to cast the curse, and I'd no idea that it housed and sustained the curse until you found it. My—she fled to who knows where. She could be hiding in the human world, for all I know, where she lost the necklace in her flight. I can only imagine that casting a curse of that magnitude must have resulted in more power than even she could control." Armand's face flickered into view, and I found him watching me with a softened expression.

"Is Tristan the only one who can leave the castle?" I asked.

"No one else wishes to, or is brave enough to try. We come from one of the farthest corners of fey country, and most of us have never interacted with humans. The tales of your people's cruelty are enough to keep us inside."

"Are tales of human cruelty truly that terrible?"

"Yes. You begin wars and plunder other lands, enslave your own people and dispose of your rulers with bloody malice. Those are no mere tales but facts. Is that not cruelty?"

"And the fey are peaceful?" I scoffed, feeling somewhat nettled that he should make a laundry list of our human failings—accurate though they may be. "I have heard otherwise."

"Oh, we have conflicts, our own sharpnesses. But we all keep to the same code. Very few of us break it. The same cannot be said for humans."

And here I was, breaking a family code of sorts so that my family might survive. "You said you cannot leave the castle. Is that part of your code?"

"I become all but invisible in sunlight. If I step outside the castle, everything slips through my hands. I can't hold so much as a flower petal in the gardens. I can do no good out there." He sounded angry now, though the anger seemed to be directed at himself. I remained silent. And if it were true, there was no way he could have been in the graveyard, just as he'd claimed yesterday.

His next words were businesslike and his tone guarded.

"Enough of codes and cruelty. I can assure you that you'll be safe performing double alchemy as the curse was not intended for you. Please, let us find out if your magic can do as you claim."

I thought briefly about the nausea from my last casting, but I brushed the thought away and promised myself I could manage such a small inconvenience.

The footsteps brought a glow descending the steps as Tristan returned. He held a burning candle in each hand.

"Tristan, in the future you will be more forthcoming," Armand demanded. The coldness in his tone surprised me. "I may belong in the dark, but our guest does not."

"As you say, my lord." Tristan bowed his head.

"And you will try to make conversation. Otherwise Beauty will believe we are as cruel and coarse as the tales make us out to be."

"Please don't ask too much of me, my lord, or I may be forced to look elsewhere for employment." I could barely make out Tristan's dry expression in the candlelight, but his gently humorous tone could not have been more different from the prince's delivery. Their exchange struck me as odd. But the same light further obscured the prince's form and left only a sparse outline. I almost wished Tristan hadn't brought the candles, as if the dark might explain the source of the prince's animosity and all the secrets he seemed to hold.

My attention went to a small table where Tristan's candles cast a warm glow on the crimson stones. The thrill of performing double alchemy mingled with pride as I stretched my hands over the necklace. I closed my eyes, aware of two sets of eyes on me as I began.

My fingers tingled. The familiar pull of magic increased as I envisioned the second stone stretching, separating, becoming two. My skin grew clammy in the cold air. I strained, feeling out how this stone was different, and encountered the same resistance sooner than last time. I fought to keep my breath steady and my mind focused, but once again I had the sensation of flipping over. Nausea roiled like an ocean in my stomach. I gritted my teeth against a scream of panic, willing everything in me to focus even as the resistance of the curse crashed against me, tossing me about. I was in control, I told myself; I knew how to do this. When the telltale *plink* sounded in my ears, my relief broke the strength holding me together. Instead of releasing the stone calmly in one smooth movement like I had imagined, I staggered back to my current situation, turning just in time to vomit on the floor instead of the table.

Damn it, I thought. So much for impressing the prince and his prickly servant with my finesse.

"I'm fine," I insisted shakily, taking the towel handed to me. It was incredibly soft and sweetly scented and made me feel guilty for wiping my sick with it.

"You should have told me that your magic affects you in this way," came Armand's voice.

"I was not planning on losing my breakfast in your exalted presence, my lord," I snapped, humiliated. "And it isn't my magic. It's that wretched curse." True, double alchemy had always offered a resistance, but I'd found it a welcome challenge. The additional resistance, nausea, and the spinning-upside-down sensation were new. My limbs felt like dead weights. I gripped the table edge to keep from toppling over in fatigue, noting that the first stone had not even caused this much difficulty for me.

"I meant you should have what you require for your task. There is no weakness in acknowledging that magic takes a toll on you. It does for the fey as well."

Armand's voice was serious, kind even, but I was in no mood to be reminded of my own weakness. "Do not patronize me."

Someone spoke words I did not hear as I fought to stay upright. "Tristan has gone for some refreshment. Not to insult you, of course, but for me. I require sustenance for the task of bearing up under your sharp tongue."

I was too tired to respond to his sarcasm. Without warning, the fatigue overwhelmed me and I toppled boneless toward the floor, only to be stopped by a strong pair of arms wrapped around my shoulders and waist. My eyes fell shut.

"I must now further insult your pride," came Armand's voice near my ear. The sarcasm was gone, leaving his voice soft. "As I am unable to conjure fainting couches, I shall have to make do."

Some feeble protest against my own weakness rose in my mind, made a valiant effort, and died. I stood on the brink of sleep, about to fall into the abyss, and yet a fey prince's arms kept me back. Warm, very strong arms, by the feel of them. I smelled the usual fey magic that bled through everything here, both sweet and sharp, and underneath that was a scent reminiscent of late summer nights and bright stars, both distant and mingled in my own blood.

"Impossible," I murmured. Armand said something, though this time I did not hear him. I seemed to be floating in a gentle current. Moments later, I was lifted and placed gently on something horizontal and soft, the consistency of clouds. Everything faded. I was floating, blissful and forgetful.

5. Shademint and Chamomile

A pleasant sleep was not to be, however. Just as I drifted into dreamland, a sharp smell snatched me back. I awoke with a yelp.

The darkness had receded somewhat, enough for me to see that Tristan stood over me with a tiny silver bottle and a gleam in his eye.

"I've never had to clean vomit before," he said.

"Add it to your list of accomplishments, then," I said, struggling to sit up. My throat was dry, my mouth terribly unpleasant. Heat flooded my face as I remembered the prince's nearness and how awful I must have smelled. Armand had smelled like—well, like something impossibly good that I could not name. I cleared my throat loudly. "I'm surprised you resorted to something as mundane as smelling salts," I said, nodding at the silver bottle. "Would you not have preferred something better than human methods?"

"I did consider a jolt of magic." Tristan's eyes flickered with humor, though his face was stolid as ever. "But that would hardly be hospitable for someone who weakened the curse. And the prince dissuaded me."

"He considered nothing of the kind," came the prince's voice.

I rose to my feet, glancing around for Armand. I had been lying on a gold silk divan, and around me I saw

50

familiar heavy tapestries, shadows, and a table displaying the same beautifully carved game we had played yesterday. In one of the nearby chairs sat a familiar shadow.

"She returns to consciousness," said Armand. "Tristan, you may leave."

As the door shut, I took my seat in the opposite chair and tried not to stare at the Ward game. It almost made me salivate.

"It worked, then?" I asked, tearing my eyes from the game as Tristan's words slowly sank in. The lighting in the room hadn't changed, yet the prince's form was easier to see even if his features were not. "My double alchemy weakened the curse?"

"It did. But first, please, enjoy some refreshment," my host said, a shadowy hand gesturing in the direction of another small table I had not noticed. A warm, tantalizing fragrance wafted from two cups, and various intricate delicacies sat on a silver plate. "Have no fear. You will not be forced to remain here if you eat this food."

I considered this in light of what I'd heard about fey food. He must have known the tales, for he said, "Dear Beauty, how would I endure your anger if I trapped you here? You have my word that I won't keep you against your will."

To my surprise I found I wanted to believe him. But was that simply because I had been briefly won over by his eyes that were now invisible to me, his voluntary vulnerability, or—I hated to admit it—because he had caught me when I fell? But my pride in my own strength was still wounded, and I would not allow myself to eat or drink anything, despite the terrible taste in my mouth.

"No thank you. I'd just as soon get on with it. The curse is breaking, and—"

"For gods' sake, woman. Have you so little belief in my hospitality? I need your help, though it pains me to say it.

Drink something. You must need to wash out that pretty mouth of yours. I cannot say that you smell exactly pleasant at the moment."

My blood boiled at this. "You don't like people rejecting your help, do you," I replied. "You enjoy being the one to give out favors. I'm beginning to wonder if you resent my help with this curse. Maybe you would rather break it all on your own."

"I should," he returned with vehemence. "I alone am to blame for it."

"Yet your self-blame has gotten you nowhere," I said.

The shadow towered over me suddenly, drawing my gaze up. Then he strode into the shadows in one quick stride and emitted a grunt of frustration. It was an odd sight, a shadow moving in this room of shadows, but I felt more triumphant than anything. I'd found a nerve at last. Now he understood how it felt to have his innermost thoughts exposed.

"How do you do that?" Armand asked. "How do you see through me? I thought I was indecipherable."

I nearly snorted a laugh. "My lord, your words and your voice give too much away for that." But my conscience chided me in my older sister's voice, as it often did. There was no time to waste arguing. A sense of guilt forced me to admit how foolish my behavior was. As I had only just mentioned, this necklace affected the welfare of many people both fey and human. Armand and I needed this partnership—a thought that surprised me. This was not a dare; he would not leave me in a graveyard and fail to grant me what I had fought for, as those boys had years ago.

I picked up one of the steaming cups and inhaled the fragrance. It smelled of shademint and chamomile, both of which Patience grew in her herb garden. I took a tentative sip. The warm, clean-scented tea felt like a taste of home, a humble reminder of all at stake.

"It's very good," I said. "The tea. I'm sorry. Arguing doesn't serve us."

The tea underwent my full inspection, and I heard the chair creak when Armand sat back down.

"Is that why you are harsh with Tristan?" I asked softly, without spite. "You can only blame yourself so much before it spills out onto others, and he is your nearest target."

The only sound to break the silence that followed was a sigh. "You're right," he admitted. "He doesn't deserve my bitterness. It has been . . . interminable, this uselessness. Having to rely on one person."

"Poor Tristan. I doubt it's been pleasant for him, either," I said dryly. "You want to help? You need mine. We share the same goal. What if I put aside my suspicion, and you your self-sufficiency?"

"It sounds as if you are suggesting we trust one another."

"I was thinking of a truce, my lord."

He chuckled. "I was right in thinking we would find something else to amuse ourselves with. But this isn't a game, is it?"

"No," I replied. "It isn't."

"In fact"—the prince hesitated—"if the aftereffects of performing double alchemy were worse this time, I fear the largest stone may pose even more of a challenge."

"I won't stop now," I said.

"I believe you. But this curse won't break easily, you understand. If there is anything you need, you have only to ask."

I kept my eyes on my hands as I stretched them out, tapping nervously on my knees. The urge to help fairly emanated from him like some kind of aura, yet he was waiting for me to express my own needs rather than simply telling me what they were. "I will need . . . something to help with the fatigue. Double alchemy always makes me tired, but I suppose fey magic is different, even if it isn't directed toward me. My sister can make something for the nausea. But I don't know of anything that will lessen exhaustion."

"You will let me help you?"

I nodded, hazarding a glance up.

"I can give you a minor charm for wakefulness when you return tomorrow," he continued, "if you will not object to fey magic."

"I don't object," I murmured.

"Thank you."

He spoke as if I had granted him a pardon or a kingdom. I had the startling, heady sensation of holding some kind of great power over him, and I had no idea how I felt about it. "A minor charm doesn't sound very important," I said by way of deflection.

"But it is to me," Prince Armand replied. "I took so much pride in taking care of my people. And what can I do now? Not so much as communicate with anyone at home, while this curse troubles everyone here. Sometimes, I feel as if I truly have disappeared. Sometimes, I don't feel real."

A twinge of sympathy struck me in the heart, a sudden recognition of that sense of aloneness. Being unable to truly share my gift of double alchemy with my family felt oppressive in a way it never had before. Before, I had taken pleasure in casting on occasion my own source of secret power. But now, it felt like an old wound suddenly causing pain.

"I am indebted to you, Beauty, and happy to be so."

"The gems will settle that debt." I felt uncomfortable with the thought of us owing each other. Failed partnerships had a habit of leaving one person with far less power than the other. It was how Mother left Father when she died, and she hadn't intended for that to happen. Even in death, her memory carried a weight that made him into a kind of half-self, his gaze fixed often on something only he could see. Of course I had every intention of succeeding in this endeavor. I had my magic, and Armand had every reason to return the castle to the kingdom. Ours was a temporary partnership.

"I won't even begrudge you for assuming I will come tomorrow," I said lightly. "You are lucky I don't have commitments."

"Would you otherwise? Have commitments to anyone?"

The way he asked made me wonder what kind of commitments he meant, but I brushed the thought away.

"Only to my family. Very few other people want anything to do with me."

"That is hard to imagine."

"Remember, my lord, no one in town knows my skill, and even if they did, it would hardly make me popular."

"That isn't what I meant. And enough with 'my lord' this and that. I thought I mentioned it yesterday. In our case it should be 'Your Highness,' in fact, but I prefer just Armand."

I stood, suddenly feeling awkward and uncertain. "I should go, my—Armand," I said. "I will see you tomorrow."

For whatever reason, Tristan did not accompany me in the carriage this time. I rapped on the roof when we emerged from the woods, and the carriage obediently came to a halt. I stepped into the garden.

So the food and drink had not ensnared me, but something about today's encounter with Armand clung to me like gossamer. It was his willingness to share with me, I realized—a marked change from yesterday, an unexpected vulnerability. And despite being practically invisible, his voice held its own openness and attraction. I shook my head.

"Patience?" I called softly, approaching the kitchen door carefully. "Don't surprise me, I beg you."

With a long-suffering sigh, Patience stepped out from behind the overgrown rose bushes that bordered the back of our house. "You're later this time," she scolded, looking me up and down as if finding evidence of my transgression. A small cauldron sloshed in her hands. "What kept you? Or do I want to know?"

"My task was more challenging today. But you know I like a challenge."

"Yes, but you seem as if something *happened*," she accused.

"Nothing happened." Why tell her about vomiting on the dungeon floor of a castle and being held upright by a fey prince? A fey prince whose arms were strong and warm and— "Do I smell more of magic this time?" I squeaked.

"*So* much more. I do hope this works. If not, you shall sleep in the garden." And without further ceremony, I found myself doused once again in sharply scented water.

My bath distracted us both from my blushing, and also did as Patience promised, for that night around the fire no one noticed anything amiss. But the smell of magic remained palpable to me, even among the everyday smells of Clotilde's tea, Father's pipe, and the firewood burning in the grate, so I had to trust Patience's assessment and my family's lack of comment.

"Beauty, where did you go today? To town, was it?" Father asked.

Patience coughed into her tea. I shot her a warning glare over the knot of thread I was unraveling for Charity. Clotilde began pounding on Patience's back with vigor, until my eldest sister waved her off with a croak of protest.

"I walked to Lowbridge," I said, naming another town not too far away. The lie sat uneasily on my tongue, as if it might expose me at any minute.

Charity glanced up from her work. "Lowbridge? Why?"

"Oh, looking for work." Not entirely a lie, since I was exchanging labor for precious stones.

"Well, I also went to Lowbridge today looking for work," Charity said. "And I didn't see you, Beauty." Thanking me, she took the thread from my hand and sewed another tiny, precise stitch. Even as I worried she would uncover my lie, I thought it a shame that no baby would ever appreciate such detail in a blanket. "But that is because I went to the grocer's, and I doubt you went there."

Clotilde began tutting at us. Father was frowning and tugging his ear as he did when unsure of whom to scold, and Patience looked murderous.

"Well! No one talks, is that it?" said Father. "Even my daughters, one to another? Charity, *cara ragazza*, why would you go all that way? Why not sell your beautiful roses here instead of traipsing the countryside like a beggar girl?"

"Because no one here will buy them, *Papà*." Charity's mouth worked and her smooth features pinched with growing agitation. "Oh, I know I've grown them for my own amusement. My magic is not so very strong, and Patience can't make potions from roses. I heard it at the market yesterday, from the butcher and tavern keeper."

"What did you hear?" Father whispered.

"They say we are fey cursed." The silence that followed Charity's words felt like the moment before a storm breaks out. "Yes, Patience, even your Laurine has heard the rumors, not that anything could keep her from you. I must walk to Lowbridge and do something with myself."

Charity's eyes were bright and her breathing fast as she glanced around at us. She was as kind as her name suggested, even more than people knew. But what others didn't know was that under the right circumstances, her anger could spark and catch like a fire.

"I think you are being brave, if foolish," I said, noting the challenge in her eye. With a shaking breath, she returned my remark with a half-grateful, half-irritated shrug of her shoulders, but she remained rigid in her seat.

"More foolish, if you ask me." Clotilde poured herself another cup of tea. "But you are grown girls. Remember that, Giacamo. You cannot stop them."

"My own house revolts against me," said Father, attempting humor but looking sad. "Well. But if this town says so—very well, Amore, Bellezza. But go together next time; that way is safer. And if anyone says anything about fey cursed again, after what happened to your mother—"

He stopped himself and readjusted in his chair with a grumble.

The atmosphere brightened when Laurine entered a few minutes later, but even her welcome presence couldn't dispel the new undercurrent that left us all unsettled. I sent Patience a look that said *I'll speak to you later*. I knew by the set of her jaw that she was still unhappy, and I did not blame her.

My sisters were saints. Patience, for her brews and for keeping my secrets. She walked Charity to town the next day. And Charity, tender, timid Charity, for telling everyone what she was attempting to do. I felt a stab of guilt the following morning. The carriage took me into the woods after my sisters' departure, and I dulled my uneasiness with the reminder that my lies would pay off in the end. Kind and determined as she was, Charity's skills would not earn enough to pay off our house, not when we had a week left to find the money.

The market wasn't the only place that had caught wind of Father's loss. Our bank had sent the letter early that morning: if we couldn't pay the remaining mortgage on the house in the next seven days, we would lose everything. I was more determined than ever to keep my course no matter how it flew in the face of our family's unspoken codes. If the results would keep us under our own roof, what did the means matter?

It seemed that some codes, I mused as the castle came into view, were meant to be broken.

6. The Council

My footsteps echoed sharply on the marble floors of a long, vaulted hallway. Tristan had not met me at the castle entrance, so I had ascended the stairs alone, found a door that I hoped was the right one, and found myself before the grand entrance to an unfamiliar room. Tristan's voice came from within the partly open double doors. Well, at least I'd found someone familiar. I stepped through the doors and into a room where rows of raised wooden seats ran all around the circular walls. Everything was paneled in dark, gleaming wood. There were at least two other entrances, and I remained hidden from view of the handful of fey people whom I could see. They were all tall and extraordinarily beautiful.

"Stop evading us, councilman du Blanc. We have a right to the truth!"

The booming male voice came from my right, but it echoed throughout the vast, domed ceiling above. Murmurs arose and fell in response to this demand. I wondered how many people were in the room, as it seemed most sat out of my sight.

"If there is a human here in our midst, then why has Prince Armand told us nothing?" came a woman's stentorian voice. She was one of the council members I could see. Graying at the temples, her skin a brown so dark it was almost black, she was a formidable-looking woman whose gaze was fixed on something to my left. A plaque bearing the name *Daphne de Lune* adorned the rail in front of her. I leaned deeper into the shadows, curious and alert. Among many things, I had never known the fey had last names.

"It's too strange, too out of the ordinary, for us to believe the prince would do such a thing," the councilwoman said.

"That is my point!" came the first voice. "Why keep this a secret if, as you say, Tristan du Blanc, it is for our good? What can a human woman do for us?"

There was such bitter spite in that voice that I cringed against the wall.

"As I've said, du Matin, the prince wanted to tell you when he had something to share." Tristan sounded as if he'd had this conversation many times before. His calm and self-controlled voice belied his weariness, and the atmosphere was thick with tension. "And as I have said, this afternoon, he will."

Poor Tristan, I thought. Not only was Armand bitter toward him, but the councilman seemed in the midst of every conflict in the castle. I began composing a very long scolding worthy of Patience's invention for the absent shadow prince.

"Princess Soline would never have kept something like this from us. She would have handled our situation with far more skill," said du Matin. Murmurs of agreement and resistance rose from the councillors.

"Princess Soline is the reason we are in exile," Tristan replied sharply. "Du Matin, you are weary. Rest until Prince Armand calls the council together this afternoon unless you want to be strong-armed into your chambers."

After a taut silence, the dark-haired fey woman spoke. "Listen to reason, Gabriel. If this afternoon provides less than satisfactory answers, we will reconsider—"

"No, Daphne." Desperation clawed at du Matin's voice. "We have waited a whole year." His voice rose, shaking as he spoke like one making a formal declaration. "I demand Prince Armand du Soir answer us now, or we make him do so by whatever means necessary."

Commotion exploded in the room. The scraping of chairs and the pattering of feet suggested something dire for Tristan, if not Armand. Alarmingly, many seemed in favor of Gabriel's demand. I didn't know why Armand wasn't there himself, but this volatile crowd was too much for Tristan alone. I steeled myself and ran into the center of the room.

"Listen to me!" I shouted. "Here is your answer!"

I had to shout repeatedly before they all saw me, and twice more before silence fell. The magnitude of my actions settled on me in the face of so many regal, stern fey staring down at me. Most stood tense and bore expressions of anger or desperation. Tristan was looking at me with a kind of horror. With effort I calmed my breathing.

"The prince and I are working together to break the curse," I said, my steady, clear voice belying my racing heart. "I don't know why Armand isn't here right now, but if Tristan promised your prince will speak with you, then he will."

"Listen to how she speaks his name so boldly." I recognized Gabriel du Matin. He looked young, handsome with piercing blue eyes, sharp cheekbones, and golden hair that fell to his shoulders. Like all fey, he had pointed ears, but he stood on the shorter side as the fey go. His gaze was even more pointed as he glared at me, but I returned his stare boldly. "So our prince has grown so weak that he consorts with a human? Did he send this human wench in his stead? We don't trust humans. This one belongs in the dungeon until we learn everything."

Pandemonium broke loose as several fey surged toward the center of the room. Tristan was shouting over them, unheard. He tried to reach me, but two fey men blocked his path with graceful malevolence. I ducked as hot and pungent magic sizzled past my ear. Anger buzzed in my veins, but the smell of fey magic had grown stronger, bitter, reminding me that double alchemy was useless here. I shouted for Tristan, wishing I could help him, when an instant later he vanished.

The angry cries faltered, changed, and rose again. I noted that some of them, Daphne among them, began drawing the others back and trying to reason with them. But those closest to me were gaining fast. I would never outrun these tall, lithe people who were far more powerful than I.

Something closed over my wrist. I tried to jerk away and found myself held fast; a familiar voice said in my ear, "I must bruise your pride once again, Beauty," and then an arm came round my waist, a familiar darkness pressed against my side, and I felt as if my soul was snatched from my body.

Sudden light blazed around me, illuminating flashes of color and strange, incomprehensible sights. I stumbled on uneven ground, but Armand's arm tightened, steadying me. Then everything came into focus.

We stood in a small, enclosed courtyard. Other than the initial disorientation, our sudden removal left no trace of ill effects upon my body or mind.

The pressure left my waist and my hand. "Stay here," Armand said, and then he was gone.

I glanced around. The courtyard lay half enshrouded in shadow, covered in moss and strange flowers that grew from the top of the wall to the ancient, split cobblestone floor. There appeared to be no way out of this place, but that hardly mattered. Something odd occupied my thoughts, mixed in with the lingering, distracting sensation of Armand's arm around me. I waited for him to return.

I had paced miles' worth of distance when Armand finally reappeared. He sank wearily onto a stone bench against the shadow side of the wall, his head in his hands.

"What happened, Armand? Are you all right?" I wanted to touch him in my excitement and relief, but his silence worried me.

"It's the council I worry about." He sighed and rubbed his face. "They're placated for now, but they've never been so agitated. We had to force one of the councilmen into his chambers. And before you ask, Tristan is safe. He disappeared some distance away when he knew he was outnumbered."

I felt no small relief for Tristan. The prince, however, seemed anything but relieved. Dropping his hands, he clenched them at his side and lifted his head. His jaw set, his eyes dark, and his brows lowered, I could see the tension in every line.

And that was just it. He was visible in daylight when he wasn't supposed to be.

Certainly, the wall cast him in shadow, but I could see him plainly despite a lingering faintness about him. He was dressed in loose shirtsleeves and black trousers, accentuating the broad angles of his shoulders that tapered down to a slender waist and long legs. I cleared my throat and fidgeted. He looked at me suddenly, his expression growing inquisitive.

"I can see you," I blurted out, partly to cover my wide-eyed gawking. In reply he stretched out his arm, examining it as if it were a new appendage, flexing his long fingers as if testing neglected muscles. How strange it must be for him to never see himself. Apparently, he could now. His eyebrows lifted in surprise.

"You can't," he replied slowly.

Hesitantly, I sat down next to him. "I can see you," I repeated, "and not only that, but the sunlight caught your shoulder when you first brought me here. It was plain as day. Didn't you say you are only visible in complete darkness?"

"Yes. And even then, I flicker like a candle at best." A line appeared between his brows. "And now here I am, more visible than I have been in a year."

"And you aren't flickering. You see? The curse continues to weaken. You and everyone here will return home soon."

"So it would appear." He sounded so unguarded, so surprised, as if understanding the implications for the first time. "I can still hardly believe it."

"It just proves that my double alchemy skills work. That, you should believe in." Pride and happiness bubbled up within me and made me bolder. I stood up. "Why stay in the shadows? Come, Armand."

The fey prince looked from my outstretched hand to my eyes.

I hadn't really known what I was doing until his fingers wrapped around mine, and the weight and smoothness of them reminded me that, despite being a fey prince, he was still very much like me. And he was letting me lead him into the sun, where until now he had been invisible, insubstantial.

Sometimes I don't feel real, he had said yesterday. I wanted to banish that for him forever.

"I've got you," I said gently, taking his hesitation for uncertainty. I had mistaken the distance between us. When he stood, he remained in the shade of the castle wall. "Come on," I coaxed, stepping back and drawing him with me. Sunlight fell across his face and revealed his features— faded, but steadily visible; he was no ephemeral wisp. I found myself looking directly up at him. The golden sunlight of a summer's midday bathed us both and turned his eyes to molten bronze.

"Can you still see me?" he asked softly, as if he were afraid of the answer.

"Yes." I cleared my throat, silently cursing the flush that suffused my face. I tugged at his hand in a half-hearted effort to make him look at himself. "Look at yourself. You're much more visible. You aren't flickering at all."

Would I be able to make him fully visible again? He certainly felt solid, as he had when he'd caught me yesterday, only this time I was fully awake and aware of standing flush against his chest. Neither of us could look away.

"I'm in your debt," Armand said. "And I'm happy for it."

The thought was no longer unpleasant. The warmth and nearness of him made me feel light-headed so that my voice sounded scratchy when I answered. "Don't be ridiculous. This is a partnership. And you appeared in time to rescue me from an angry mob. So, I declare us even."

He smiled. "I think I prefer being in your debt."

The flush deepened in my cheeks. This was too much; I stepped back so that he released me and grasped for any kind of misdirection. "Where were you this morning? When the council met."

Armand retreated into the shadows; I resisted the urge to pull him back to me, a stupid contradiction to my previous action.

He heaved a frustrated sigh. "My room disappeared."

"It what?"

"It disappeared. When I opened the door to attend the council, there was no hallway, no way to exit, nothing. Remember, everything within this castle fluctuates in some way. Rooms appear on different floors, and sometimes vanish altogether, only to reappear again, sometimes weeks later. People's tempers rise and fall, as you saw; it's not always safe for me to be near them. Only Tristan remains the same. He has far too much to do on his own. It shouldn't be this way." Weariness and guilt showed on his face. "I doubt even Soline understood how powerful her spell was when she cast it."

"Princess Soline?" I remembered the name from the council room. "She is one you rejected?"

The prince grimaced. "Yes."

"Were you married?" I poked the toe of my shoe into a dent in the stone, where dirt encouraged tiny plants to sprout up, little pink things I had never seen in any garden. Rulers married purely for political reasons all the time. I thought of Soline in a loveless marriage and found myself torn between pity for her and other unpleasant feelings too complicated to parse at the moment.

Armand shook his head. "No. Our kingdom traditionally has two rulers at all times; marriage is not a necessity. Maybe I should have married her. I might have learned to love her, and no one would have been exiled."

"You can't believe this is all your fault, Armand," I said briskly. "Prince or no, even you must stop taking on burdens not your own."

"I wish it were easier."

"So do I," I said wryly. "Your propensity to not share burden with others is unpleasant. But see, you're sharing this task now. We're working together, aren't we?"

"Yes," he said. "But this is no burden."

Armand looked as though he would say something. He brushed a hand along his jaw and quirked his head, a warm expression filling his eyes.

"And what of you, Beauty? I'm beginning to think we are alike. Do you carry more than you should, or does your family share your burdens?"

"Some." I shrugged. "I would rather spare them as much as possible."

"Hm." He scrutinized me further until I dropped my gaze. Then he stood.

"Are you ready to continue?" Smiling, he held out his arm for me.

I nodded and returned his smile. Gods, he was attractive. But I went in without taking his arm. I was a fool if I thought a fey prince would consider me as a partner in anything more intimate, no matter how charming his manners toward me might be or how much I might want him to see me as more than a necessary partnership.

7. The Third Ruby

Armand revealed a wooden door hidden beneath pink-flowered vines. Once we entered the cool, dark interior, he became a vague shadow beside me. I wanted to reach out and touch him but held back and scolded myself instead. Through rooms and hallways I had never seen and would never remember, he led me to the plain door and the velvet-heavy room, dim and stuffy as before.

The sofa I had lain upon yesterday remained. The ruby necklace lay upon the table where the Ward game had been. The whole atmosphere was very sleepy, and I wished more than ever I could see my one companion in the room.

Strange, I thought, that I was alone in the room with a fey prince and comfortable, whereas I'd found most other human men, save my father, to be less than easy company.

"Why should we keep the room dark?" I asked briskly. "You are visible in the light. And even if that was an aberration, I'd still prefer to see my surroundings clearly." Without waiting for an answer, I swept aside a curtain, sending dust motes flying and sunlight in.

"Hm." Armand's voice hummed above my shoulder. He was not terribly close, but a flame sparked in my body nonetheless. "There seems to be a problem."

I glanced over my shoulder and saw what he meant. Rather, I saw he was not so much as the shadow I expected, but no longer visible at all.

"I wonder—" His breath stirred my hair. "May I touch you?"

I nodded, pulse throbbing. Warm fingers closed gently around my forearm. The brush of his thumb sliding down my wrist into my palm elicited a shiver, and he took my hand.

"Beauty," he said, "look."

I turned around to see our joined hands, visible. Long pale fingers wrapped around my darker, rather stubby ones, and Armand was entirely visible. When he released me briefly, he vanished, and I felt a kind of hungry relief when he took my outstretched hand again and reappeared. I drank in the sight of him and found his heated gaze on me.

"Why the inconsistency? You were visible in the courtyard without touching me." My pulse was no longer throbbing; it was roaring.

"It will not break smoothly or neatly, but the curse is weakening nonetheless. You are weakening it." His eyes held mine, then dipped to my mouth.

I couldn't trust myself to speak. The seconds seemed to stretch into infinity. I fought the urge to step closer and had just given in when, Armand stepped back from me with a sharp inhale.

"I shouldn't keep you." He sounded regretful, though I wasn't sure of the cause, and he still held my hand.

Reluctantly I released him as we took a place on either side of the table where I gazed at the ruby necklace. The large middle jewel looked like a well of blood, reminding me that this would be the most difficult casting yet.

"You said you would have a spell to fight against the effects of the curse," I said. Patience had indeed forced a horrible potion down my throat that seemed more likely to induce vomiting than prevent it, but just now I was trying to prevent fevered visions of falling into his arms from commanding my thoughts. I failed spectacularly.

"Yes. It's a bracelet I fashioned. Here, hold out your hand."

Something cool slipped over my hand, and I inhaled quickly as Armand brushed the sensitive skin along my wrist again. His gaze was trained on my hand—or the bracelet— as he flickered into view for a moment far too brief.

"It will not make you totally immune to the effects of your own magic, since the charm works primarily on fey magic. But it should help protect you from the most exhausting effects."

I glanced down at the bracelet on my arm. Now visible, it looked to be made of some kind of thin, gleaming wire, neither gold nor silver, woven together in a loose braid cool against my skin: another reminder of what was at stake, what I was risking. The last of the frenzied heat ebbed from my body, and I sobered. It was time to get in control of myself. "Thank you, Armand."

"Stop, if it becomes too difficult."

As I shut my eyes, I let everything else fade and focused on envisioning the cursed necklace in front of me. Immediately the largest stone at the center throbbed, and my hands tingled painfully. I could feel the bracelet burning cold on my right wrist, emanating repellant waves that pushed against the energy trapped in the ruby. Slowly, the gemstone began to expand, to pull apart. All was going well; I felt a flare of triumph even as I braced against the coming resistance. Then the energy battling between bracelet and gem fluxed mightily. Nausea rose and fell, rose and fell, while I fought to keep my breathing even. Two stones strained apart. They had almost separated when the tug of war lurched so fiercely I couldn't be sure which direction the fight went, or where I was; instead of being flipped

71

upside down, I was falling, tumbling, head over heels into an endless abyss. Someone cried out. It took every ounce of my strength to keep the gems fixed in my mind's eye. I was losing control, and the gems wavered in view.

With a final pull, the gems split apart, disappearing from my vision. I continued to fall without knowing if my eyes opened or not.

"That's enough, Beauty. Stop! Do you hear me? Beauty!"

Spinning over me like a child's top, Armand's face came into view. I clutched at something soft. Nausea rose once more and fell, pulling my stomach and energy down with it, and darkness took me once more.

The curtains were closed again. The light of one candle flickered dimly to my right. I sat up slowly, my limbs still heavy with fatigue, and searched for Armand. The room seemed totally empty.

When I stood, I realized the true source of the darkness. The curtains remained open, revealing the deep, star-struck night sky that arced over stately trees and gardens.

"It's night," I said aloud. "They will be worried sick about me." I wobbled to the door just as it opened and Armand's faint form entered, visible again in the gloom, followed by Tristan. Both carried trays of food.

Tristan answered my question before I could speak. "I just sent a letter to your family, stating that you have gone to stay with an aunt in Green Hill."

"But how do you know about Aunt Meg?"

"Your sister Patience was most helpful." He set down the tray. "She also threatened to put a spell on me if I did not return you in time. You can be sure I will keep my word." With rare a smile, Tristan bowed and left the room.

Imagining such an encounter brought a brief smile to my face as well.

I went to the table where the necklace lay and saw that I had, indeed, made a second large stone, and that a large crack ran down the center of the original. At least I'd succeeded in that regard, even if exhaustion had overtaken me. I was uninjured. Armand's bracelet still encircled my wrist, now the same temperature as my skin.

"What time is it?" I asked.

"Nearly ten. I tried to wake you, but it was impossible. So I sent Tristan to make arrangements."

I was grateful my family shouldn't worry about me, but now I had other predicaments that hardly allowed me to notice the unease in his voice. Such as staying with a fey prince I found not only attractive, but someone I could see myself forming a deep attachment to. But such a thing was impossible. This was a temporary arrangement, and would end with him returning to his country, whereas I would remain firmly planted in the human realm—hopefully still housed.

With this thought fixed in place, I turned to Armand. "I am grateful to him for that. My family would be far more than worried if everyone knew where I really am."

He smiled a bit abstractly and gestured toward the trays of food on the larger table. "You must be hungry. Will you eat?"

"Only if you will eat with me," I said, and this time, when we sat in the chairs where we had first made one another's acquaintance, instead of a game of Ward we shared a meal.

The food was a delicious feast of both simple and complex dishes, some I recognized. I ate with abandon. Armand smiled at my enthusiasm, chuckling and teasing me about my simple human tastes until his comments took a more serious turn.

"I think it might be best if you left the necklace alone."

"Why would you say that?" I asked, surprised. "I succeeded in doubling the largest stone. Did something happen with the curse?"

He shook his head.

"Then what is it?" I asked. "Surely the worst is behind us."

"I'm not entirely sure that is the case." Armand set down his fork and wiped his hands on a napkin, playing with it for a while. The stark white of the fabric looked odd against his barely opaque hands. "You were so deeply asleep this time. Ten hours. I was worried for you, Beauty."

I leveled my gaze at him. "I am fine, thanks no doubt to your charm. And your care. I don't wish to take your concern lightly, but you understand the importance of this for me."

He frowned. "Can you not duplicate the gems you already have?"

"Gems can only be duplicated once. I've tried, you see."

The line between his brows deepened. "I may have understood your desire to earn your reward, but this—"

"No." I shook my head vehemently. "I will finish this, Armand. Do not disrespect me by offering otherwise. Is there another reason you want to send me away before our agreement is fulfilled?"

"There isn't," he said quickly. When he reached for my hand, I placed it in his without hesitation, relishing the unnecessary gesture and the undeniable thrill it caused me.

Armand was not the first man whose touch I had ever wanted. Nor was this the first time he had touched me, and yet I suddenly wanted him in a way I'd never wanted anyone else before. I wanted to say something alluring, something that would tell him of my own longing, but nothing would come to mind. He watched me with a warmth that seemed to spread throughout my whole being and made my heart flutter.

"So you have no one else to share your double alchemy with, though you love your family dearly." Armand looked down at our entwined fingers, and I wondered at how he hadn't withdrawn, how this small intimacy felt so natural and so new at the same time. He leaned forward, his brown eyes earnest and searching. "What happened to make you hide this part of yourself?"

What happened? No one had asked me that before. At his gentle question, the strange sadness returned.

"My mother died five years ago," I began. "My father was so bereft that he nearly ran his business aground. Patience comforted him, and I comforted Charity and saw to Father's records and correspondence, trying to keep business going. I made so many mistakes at first that we lost a lot of money anyway. To pay the bills, I had to use my magic for the first time in many years. Until then it was only a source of amusement." I smiled sadly. Mother had thought my double alchemy amusing, harmless, even special. But then she was gone, and it became a secret resource in a time of desperation. "Father didn't know, but I heard him talking once about how, when Mother was pregnant with me, she made a trade with a fey woman in the city. In Father's mind, it's all connected: double alchemy, Mother's trade, the fey. Maybe even her death. I knew then I could never perform my magic around my family again."

Armand rubbed his thumb across my hand, but this time it was comforting, tender. Still, it made my pulse jump. I felt vulnerable and uncertain. "I doubt you have ever had to hide your magic," I said, wanting to hear him say something.

"You're right," he said. "It was always a public thing. My parents are both gone, but I think I will always carry two things from them: a sense of their love, and a persistent fear that if I do not maintain their hopes for me, I will have failed them utterly." Armand leaned back in his chair as his eyes took on a distant quality. "They were commoners, ordinary fey with no connections to royalty. Because of their belief in me and hard work, I caught the notice of the royal academy and soon joined the ranks of those training to be potential rulers of Clear Star. My parents always prepared a feast for me when I visited home; they were so proud of me, without ever being pretentious. I felt so loved, so invincible because of them." He laughed sadly. "Not until after their deaths did I discover that they had gone without so much. Those feasts meant they sometimes went hungry. When they dismissed my offers to help with repairs—a rotten floorboard, a broken door hinge—I told myself that if I was crowned the first thing I would do would be to buy them a new home. I was grieved that they hadn't lived to see me ascend the throne, but I was furious that they hadn't let me help them." He glanced at me ruefully. "I am sorry, Beauty. You didn't ask to hear all this."

It was my turn to squeeze his hand. "I am glad you told me," I said truthfully, though I could hardly imagine what it would be like to have two parents as supportive as Armand's. Our hands remained intertwined. How unexpected, I thought, to come from such different backgrounds and yet still feel at home sharing losses and griefs we hadn't shared with anyone else. "We both have our reasons for doing what we must. Now I understand yours."

"Our reasons," Armand repeated. "And obligations."

The prince of Clear Star sounded resolute, yet sad. He withdrew his hand and stood, a faint form in the candlelight once again.

"I should take you to your room," he said. His face was serious as his tone, polite, as if remembering this was a business arrangement. "You'll be weary soon enough, I expect."

"No, I don't think so," I began, resisting something I could not quite name, but a yawn interrupted me. Suddenly I was tired, grumpy, and deeply disappointed.

Armand did not offer his arm when we left.

8. A Surprising Offer

Despite my ten-hour nap, sleep claimed me within minutes of sinking into the bed. At daylight I awoke and tried to make myself presentable. My dress was heavily creased and my hair a tangle of fuzzy, loose curls, but the elaborate dresser displayed a basin of water, a cake of engraved, sweetly scented soap, fresh towels, and a comb that served to make me feel refreshed.

With a fistful of hair in one hand and the comb in the other, my stomach flip-flopped at the memory of the previous night. Had Armand shown concern only for how effective I was in breaking the curse, or was it something more personal? The warmth of his gaze and his hand made my face flush, leaving me pleasantly confused—until the comb caught a snarl in my fine hair and made me yelp. I muttered a curse and tossed the comb back onto the dresser. Uncertain whether I dreaded or longed to see him, I couldn't stay in this room all day if I was to duplicate the fourth stone.

Tristan arrived at my door to say he'd bring me to breakfast. I thought of how much he must have endured in the year since the curse, and how well he had handled yesterday's uproar.

"If all council meetings are as exciting as yesterday's, you must look forward to them," I said to Tristan's straight back as we went through a door and out to a charming terrace. The sight of Armand sitting at a nearby table tripped my thoughts to a halt. He was no longer invisible in sunlight, and I felt ridiculously disappointed at the loss of a reason to touch him. "What I mean is, Tristan, I thought you handled everything with dignity."

Tristan actually smiled. True, it was a sour half smile, and he followed it with a customary remark. "And you were foolish," he replied. "But brave. Thank you for trying to help, however little it achieved."

I sat down with my shoulders squared, feeling as though I had won over the entire council myself.

"My lord, the council awaits your appearance today," Tristan said, addressing the prince. "What time will you see them?"

Armand put down the papers he had been reading and frowned. A lovely breakfast sat waiting on the table. There were flaky croissants and bright summer fruits, a steaming carafe of creamy coffee, fried eggs, and sausage, which seemed a bit much for breakfast. I sat and helped myself, feeling less like a guest and more like an awkward, hungry observer.

"As soon as possible. In an hour, if that suits everyone. And Tristan—" Armand paused to shuffle the papers unnecessarily. He sat with one ankle propped against his other knee, and I hadn't failed to notice his white shirt loose and open at the neck. "I've behaved like an ass toward you. It's the last thing you deserve. You've been carrying so many responsibilities that should have been mine, and when I could not carry out the tasks myself, I resented you for how well you did. I'm sorry."

Tristan paused before responding. "Much appreciated, my lord," he replied. "We are all ready to resume our usual way of things."

I listened to this exchange quietly, smiling at my croissant.

"Everyone except Gabriel," Tristan continued. "While the curse's ability to agitate the council seems to have lessened since yesterday"—here he acknowledged me with a nod, causing me to nearly drop my coffee cup—"Gabriel remains stubbornly opposed to you and has only gotten worse. He broke out of his rooms last night and became violent. We had to subdue him and remove him to the dungeons after he tried to attack a servant, one Juliette Ciel-Noir."

Armand's frown deepened. "Is she all right?"

"Unharmed. She was the one to stop him."

"Still, this must be addressed. We will meet in an hour, and then I'll see to Gabriel myself. And Tristan, when we've returned, you must spend a month at home with your husband. I won't take no for an answer."

Fatigue and relief showed on the councilman's handsome features as he briefly shut his eyes. "I won't argue with that, my lord." With a word of thanks from his prince, Tristan returned indoors.

Now alone with Armand, I felt uncertain of how to address him. Brow furrowed in thought, he was fully absorbed in reading through his papers, almost as if he'd forgotten I was there. But it gave me a moment of reprieve. I lifted my face to the sunshine and shut my eyes, savoring the warmth until thoughts of my sisters and father descended upon me. I wondered if Charity had found work that she liked, and whether she would stand up for herself or if her employers would take advantage of her naivete, forcing a lower pay than she deserved. I hoped Patience was not worn too thin with worry. I thought of Father, as naively hopeful as Charity in some ways, and of Clotilde, who had been with us for so long; would she return to her family if we lost our home, or would the journey be too much for her now? It seemed entirely unfair that I was relaxing in a fey castle when my family lived in worry-tinged ignorance or secret fear, even though I had only two gems left to duplicate and thus secure our future.

I opened my eyes as a thought came to mind. Regardless of how Armand saw me, I felt compelled to do something about the current situation with the council.

"Armand?"

"Yes?"

"I would also like to speak to the council."

He looked at me thoughtfully, and I thought again how much I wanted to break this spell and make him fully visible, as solid as he had felt yesterday. A fresh wave of longing swept through me and I fought to keep my thoughts on the task at hand.

"Why is that?" Armand asked. He spoke without condescension or doubt, merely curiosity.

"Since they saw me yesterday, and they already know you have kept my presence here a secret, they should see us together. Together, I mean, to answer their questions. And answer me this: why *have* you kept my presence a secret?"

He frowned. "I wanted to tell them when I had proof that our attempts were working. Duplicating the third ruby weakened the curse enough for me to be seen in daylight, and in shadows, yet I haven't found any other visible proof. And, as you saw, some of them can be especially volatile. I didn't want to risk endangering you, or causing uproar. But," he sighed, scrubbing his jaw absently, "even though I spoke to them yesterday, I should have been there for the first meeting. A disappearing room is no excuse for shirking my responsibilities."

"Let me go with you to the council. I've as much a right to be there as you."

"I could give you a few hints beforehand," Armand said slowly. I pressed my point home.

"You know better than I do how stretched thin Tristan is, and you said you need to accept help more often. I am

81

capable, Armand. Besides," I added grimly, thinking of the Ward team, "I have experience dealing with prickly groups of elitists."

Armand threw back his head and laughed. "Elitist is a fine word while the monarchy remains! But you have made your point and you are right. Beauty, I would be grateful if you accompanied me to the council. No, wait." He held up a hand. "Please come with me, but wait outside the council chamber until I have addressed them first, to explain why I kept it a secret from them in the first place. They will respond better if you join me after that. Do you accept my conditions?"

I nodded. "Yes."

"Hm. That was far too easy. I expected more of a fight from you."

"I could say the same for you," I said, allowing myself a faint smile. "Could it be that we have an influence over each other?"

"You certainly have influence over me."

Maybe it was the heat in his eyes; maybe it was the return of our banter. Either way, I could no longer remain silent about what had passed between us last night.

"Armand." I squared my shoulders and lifted my chin, stretching out my hands on my knees. "I want you to tell me if what happened last night was a game. If what passed between us was real."

I dropped my eyes, wishing I could find better words; but these were not columns of numbers or intricate Ward moves, and my other romantic encounters had been brief at best; I had little experience with this kind of thing. I stood and turned from the table, unable to remain still.

"Well, say something, so I know I haven't ruined everything," I mumbled.

"You haven't ruined anything." Armand rose and approached me. "Beauty, I wanted to say something last night. I almost did. But the more we spoke, the more I was reminded of everything pulling us in different directions. I did not want to ask something of you that was unfair and selfish. And yet, like a royal idiot, I caught myself taking liberties—a touch, lingering too long—I shouldn't have."

"Armand, you could have simply asked." I turned to meet his gaze with a small smile, feeling unaccountably shy. "Is it selfish if I want the same thing?" But my smile faltered as his words sank in, reminding me of my own unspoken thoughts: *everything pulling us in different directions.*

A number of emotions flitted across Armand's face, some of which I recognized in myself. Longing. Uncertainty. Desire. And the weight of all we carried.

"Nothing lasts forever," I said. "I do not believe it has to, to be beautiful."

He walked toward me until he stood near enough that to touch him would be the movement of a heartbeat. I could see every fine lash surrounding his brown eyes, every detail brought to starker contrast by the effects of my recent work.

"Beautiful. Yes." He brushed my cheek. "Is this what you want? A casual love affair?"

I leaned against the warmth of him and put my hands on his chest.

"I want you to stop talking and kiss me," I whispered, "or I will believe you are a royal idiot."

His breath brushed my lips as he laughed softly. "I may be yet. But it won't be for want of kissing you."

He closed the space between us and kissed me.

It felt like eternity. It felt like a moment in time. When Armand released me, I felt full of longing that burned all other desires away.

An hour later, I stood outside massive double doors bordered with massive columns of black with gold trim. The council chamber had disappeared, it seemed, so we were meeting in the ballroom. I could hear only indistinct voices through the door.

Daphne had kindly loaned me one of her gowns and a soft-bristled brush for my fine, wavy hair. She and an alarmingly cheerful maid had helped me dress. The gown was a little too long, and I felt ridiculous; but Daphne informed me, in a way that reminded me of Patience, that I would garner more respect if I dressed accordingly, offered a few choice insights regarding the council, and left me to finish dressing. Even the maid, the very same Juliette whom Gabriel had attacked, said no more than "best of luck," finished buttoning my gown, and almost danced from the room with an impish smile on her face.

And there I was, tugging at luxurious, raspberry-colored fabric and trying not to feel like a small child playing dress-up.

I could think of little else but the kiss between Armand and me. Though my lips burned with wanting to experience him again, it was like holding on to the shreds of a wonderful dream. Instead, I forced myself to remain composed and wait for the fey prince as if nothing had passed between us. At any minute, I would stand before a group of the most elegant and alarming people I had ever seen. They made the boys who had excluded me seem crude and backwards, even now as grown men. The thought made me smile.

A hand clamped down on my shoulder and spun me around. Amidst a flurry of startled disorientation, I recognized a blur of golden hair, sharp cheekbones, and a sharper glare.

"One of Soline's spies?" Gabriel hissed. His grip was iron, his eyes crazed.

"If you're looking for the meeting, it is through there," I said calmly, gesturing at the doors behind me. I was frightened, but he did not seem completely in control of himself; the curse was toying with him, and though I had no idea how he'd escaped the dungeon, I didn't want to find out what else it would take to set him off.

Not much, unfortunately. My teeth rattled in my head as he shook me hard once and seized my other shoulder.

"You're the human. I must have been right about Armand, though. If you're here, he's got to be in league with our traitorous princess."

"I promise you, he is not," I said. The man was making no sense; even his judgments regarding why I was here were inconsistent. "And in just a moment, you can speak to him yourself." I prayed that would be sooner rather than later. The man was sweating beads. If I screamed for help, I doubted anything good would come of it.

The frantic blue eyes narrowed. "Why wait a moment? I've already waited a year." With a wave of his hand the doors flew open with a resounding crash, causing one to sag at the hinges, and Gabriel dragged me through them.

I managed to regain my footing and stumble along, taking in my surroundings with a growing sense of wonder. The room looked like some kind of planetarium, with a tall, domed ceiling of glass, but instead of the bright summer sky it showed the blue depths of the ocean. The large, tapered belly of a whale passed slowly overhead, startling me so much that I almost fell.

"Gabriel!"

Armand's voice echoed in the room, authoritative and resonant. He and the other councillors stood at a large table covered in documents. Their prince and several others advanced quickly.

"Wait," I said. My voice, too, sounded loud and strange, but it was calm. "If we listen to him, he will let me go." I shook my head imperceptibly at Armand, trying to reassure him even though he must have known I spoke with more confidence than the situation warranted. He looked ready to spring any moment. The faintest tension in his features hinted at his anxiety, but the moment I made eye contact with him, he relaxed and looked at the escaped councillor.

"What do you have to say, Gabriel?" Armand asked, in a tone implying this was an ordinary meeting with non-cursed individuals. In the wavering, watery light, he looked almost as solid as everyone else.

The agitated fey blinked around the room, shifting his grip on my arm. "We've been exiled for an entire year, my lord. I demand to know why you haven't brought us home yet. You have evaded your duty in the worst way."

"Gabriel, I hear your complaints, and they are true." Armand shut his eyes briefly as he fought to keep his composure. This whole scene, I understood, was one of his worst nightmares: watching someone under his care suffer, when he had no sure way of helping. "I have evaded you all. Sometimes, in truth, it was beyond my control, but there were times I could have sought you out. I thought it would be better to address the council only when I had some kind of progress to report. That was wrong of me. I have no excuse for not speaking to you all sooner."

Gabriel seemed to notice Tristan for the first time and pointed an accusing finger at him. "You put me in the dungeons." He was trembling violently now, his grip loosening on my arm. Confusion, fear, bitterness contorted his face; he was in a fragile state, and while I could easily extract my arm and leave, I wasn't sure that would be wise. Instead I put my free hand on his shoulder.

"Gabriel, everyone here wants to go home, including me," I said. "Everyone is trying to break the curse. It has made everyone do things they wouldn't otherwise do, but everyone here has the same goal."

86

He looked at me as if seeing me for the first time. "You're human," he murmured, none of the earlier accusation in his voice. "You're the double alchemist. You're not in league with the princess?"

"I'm not in league with the princess." The poor man looked so confused and shaken now that I couldn't help feeling pity for him. His shoulders hunched, and he trembled so violently that he clutched my arm for support now. "Here," I said gently, leading him to a chair, "you've had an ordeal, my friend. Sit here and rest. We will get you some refreshment."

As Gabriel collapsed in the chair, so did the last of his resolve. He burst into the most piteous tears, crying like a child and leaning against my arm.

"My friend." Daphne had approached in a rustle of fabric, her brown eyes kind and clear. "Can you trust now that we still care for you? Can you trust us enough to hear what we have to say?"

Gabriel nodded his tear-stained face. "I'm an absolute fool who deserves to be rejected from the council."

I barely stifled a snort; Daphne shot me a warning glance. "That remains to be seen," she said. "Come, join us, and eat something. Prince Armand was telling us his progress in breaking the curse."

The contrite fey glanced up at me and finally removed his hand from my arm. "I'm terribly sorry. My behavior is appalling. Please tell me how I can make it up to you. I will offer you half my wealth, or—are you in need of a husband? I am not the best our kingdom has to offer, and I can still be hot-headed even in the best of times, but I will try, I promise, if that is what you—"

"No," I cut him off just as Armand said the same thing, with rather more force. I stood and gestured toward the table. "You can make it up to me by joining us, and by never offering either of those things again."

Gabriel straightened and inhaled shakily, his face and form regaining some of the composure I'd witnessed in the council room earlier, though with far more humility. "I would be honored."

Somehow, he sounded simple and honest rather than stuffy.

Armand and I spoke to the council about the plan, my progress with the necklace, and our expectations that double alchemy would be enough to fully break the princess's curse. And when the council adjourned and Armand escorted me out, he offered not his arm, but his hand. I took it in the sight of everyone.

There were mutters of surprise and, I thought, displeased concern.

"Ah," Gabriel said. "I see."

9. A Fleeting Bliss

As my family did not expect me until the following day, there was no rush to duplicate the next ruby. Armand and I walked through the garden in golden afternoon light, eating mild cheeses, fresh tomatoes, and figs as we walked. While the setting was beautiful and grand in my eyes, Armand showed me the ragged edges of the garden where everything had been torn away by the curse. Sometimes trees were split in two at these places, and the forest pressed against them as if trying to reclaim stolen space. We spoke of our families and of Clear Star. All the while he kept hold of my hand, and I allowed myself to remain in that single, sweet moment. When he pressed me against one of the stately trees beside rows of fragrant blossoms, I leaned into his kiss and found it impossible to step away.

But the sun slipped between the trees, reminding us we could no longer ignore my task. We returned indoors through shadow-crossed paths. Armand looked almost completely solid in the fading light.

"I'm not hungry yet," I replied when he asked if I wanted to eat dinner before replicating the fourth stone. It was true, because all I could think about was the constant warmth of our joined hands and how much I wanted to kiss him again. How much I wanted *him*. "And," I continued briskly, "since I will fall asleep, I'd rather bring the necklace to my bedroom."

We stopped in the doorway off the terrace where he drew me close enough to feel his heartbeat. "Do you still want me to come with you?"

I nodded, lifting my chin and brushing a strand of hair from his eyes. "Yes."

Armand needn't have worried about the difficulty of this stone; though still more taxing than any double alchemy I had performed in the human realm, the task was soon over, leaving me tired but not senseless. At least, not immediately.

I crawled into my bed, half-supported by Armand.

"I have difficulty accepting help," I began, only for him to give an annoyed chuckle that almost sounded affectionate.

"We seem to have that in common," he whispered as I settled between the sheets, his hand brushing a wayward curl from my mouth. "You are one of the strongest people I know. But now you need rest."

"I wasn't done." The bed felt heavenly, yet empty; I could not let him leave yet. "You once said you wounded my pride with your help. You don't anymore. I would happily be carried to bed by you any day, Armand."

He grunted, making me smile to hear the frustration and longing in his voice. Then he stepped away.

I grabbed his wrist. "Stay."

He inhaled slowly.

"Just one night. Please, Armand."

His hand slipped from my grasp. The bed shook slightly and I felt his warm body curl around mine, his arm draped over my side where he took my hand again. "Like this?" His breath stirred my hair.

"For now." I smiled again and shut my eyes, happy at last to let sleep overtake me.

A deep sadness invaded this moment of bliss. In another day's time, the final duplication finished, he would return to his country, and I would never see him again. What if we could find another way? My fatigued brain struggled for a solution. He could not leave his people; I could not leave my family for an unknown fey country. The sadness grew heavier, tinged with frustration, and followed me deep into sleep.

It was dark when I awoke. Brief confusion gave way to a host of other feelings. Armand lay beside me, the profile of his face with his dark lashes and delicious mouth visible in the light of a single candle. How beautiful and vulnerable he looked in sleep. I leaned closer and softly touched my lips to his.

He stirred and opened his eyes. With his smile, drowsiness burned into desire.

A deep and sudden hunger blossomed within me, the unfolding of building desire no longer kept at bay. I saw it mirrored in his eyes. I kissed him with an urgency he returned until, breathing heavily, he pulled away.

"Do you want this?" Armand whispered huskily, stroking my cheek, my hair. I shivered and nodded. He eased himself onto one elbow and drew his fingers down my arm. "I want to hear you say it. Tell me, Beauty."

"I want this. I want you."

There was only warmth and aching tension and blinding ecstasy between us, and I wanted nothing else.

Those hours held multitudes. Yet when we awoke a second time to bright skies, my anxieties returned in full force, unwanted intruders threatening to steal what we had before we lost it. Even the strength of his arms around me and the warmth of our skin pressed together only served to highlight the coming pain. Because I knew, with startling clarity, that I loved Armand. It wasn't just the physical attraction, though that had been there even before I had seen him. It wasn't just our intimacy, though that was too wondrous and delicious for words. We belonged to different classes and realms, and yet he had seen me from the start in a way that no one ever had, not even my beloved family, and I knew it was true for him, too. But if the council's reaction yesterday was any indication, yet another hindrance to our relationship existed, and the morning offered no solution.

Gently, Armand lifted my chin to look up at him. "It's too beautiful a morning to think troubled thoughts," he said, his voice gravelly with sleep. "Let me put something more pleasant on your mind."

He rolled over me and buried his face in my hair, kissing my neck until my worries melted into something ephemeral and distant. Afterward I felt serene, blissful; I almost told Armand how I felt about him, but something held me back.

"You must take better care of yourself, Armand." We lay side by side, staring up at the ceiling with our hands clasped. "When you return and Tristan enjoys his well-deserved rest, you will work yourself to death as if you learned nothing at all. Promise me that after I leave, you'll keep remembering that nothing can ever make you unworthy of others' help."

When he remained silent, I turned and was surprised to find his eyes closed, his face set in a look almost of pain. Had I overstepped the bounds of a casual love affair?

"Beauty, you have done more for me in these past three days than you know. Before you, I was furious that I couldn't do everything on my own. You showed me how beneficial an unexpected partnership can be. I am happily indebted to you. The entire kingdom is, and I will make sure they know it."

The words lanced me with bitterness like poison. Of course, he was referring to the cursed necklace, nothing more, and he should express nothing more. But oh, it still hurt. The thought of having the gratitude of thousands of fey paled in the face of Armand's lack of personal feelings for me. I did not want a casual love affair, but what else was there for us? Silently I cursed myself for getting so attached, when both of us had acknowledged yesterday that this was temporary, a physical and emotional attraction that had no future. For him, nothing had changed.

"I should go." I sat up and reached for my clothes, at once reluctant and desperate to leave. "Tomorrow, then. For the final gem."

The only indication that he wasn't fully his normal, visible self was how pale his arm looked when he reached through a shaft of sunlight for me. He sat up and kissed my hand, a gallant, formal gesture, as if he were already saying goodbye, already marking the distance that awaited us.

"Tomorrow, Beauty."

The four gems weighed in my pocket as I left the forest behind. I should have been glad that in one short day I could reassure my family that all would be as it should. We would go on living in our house, my father comfortable, my sisters happy in their gardens—although Patience was bound to marry Laurine any day once our financial crisis was well averted. The thought made me smile. I liked Laurine; she had a way about her that made the crispiest heart soften, and while Patience could never be called hard-hearted, seeing the two of them together was like watching two perfect stones blend and strengthen the other without losing any of their own shape—a sort of reverse double alchemy.

Something sounded wrong before the garden came into view. My heartbeat quickened, and I saw why: one man shouted directions while others loaded furniture into several large carts, like ants carrying off food. My mind refused to understand at first. I almost went to them and demanded to know whose furniture they were carrying away, when Charity came running out and flung herself into my arms.

"I'm so glad you're back." She'd been crying. Tears streaked her face and she was sniffing vigorously; I was alarmed to see how exhausted she looked.

"Charity, Sweet, when did they get here? Where are *Papà* and Patience?"

I put my hands on her shoulders and suddenly I was holding the young, scared Charity of five years ago, thin-shouldered and frightened at the senseless loss of our mother. Her mouth opened and shut without saying anything; her eyes looked large and her gaze distant, as if she were retreating into herself. I put one arm around her and steered her toward the kitchen door, not even caring if I smelled of fey magic. My blood boiled as I glared at the men stealing our belongings and sending my sister back to that place of helplessness and grief. One of them flew out of the kitchen door in front of us. I grabbed his coat, forcing him to halt, and noted he carried Mother's portrait.

"Give that back at once," I demanded. This couldn't be happening; I hadn't been gone a week, they were mistaken, this was all a dreadful blunder on the part of some stupid bank owner who couldn't be bothered to count properly.

"I said, give it to me," I repeated when the man merely blinked at me. "Who gave you permission to steal our belongings?"

"Mr. Xander of Larkspur bank," the oaf replied. "And we aren't stealing, miss. We have a letter. Hey, Lester! Show this girl Mr. Xander's letter!"

I was seething. I had to keep a cool head for Charity's sake, and for everyone else surely frantic inside the house. "My name is Miss Giordano," I said coolly, "and Mr. Xander will have a lawsuit on his hands if he doesn't return our things this instant."

Charity whimpered at my side. "Can't, miss." Another man sidled up, his long hair tied back and a snaky smile on his lips. He'd been the one shouting orders when I arrived. "It says he can claim what's rightfully his in a week's time *or less*, right here."

I snatched the letter and read it, then cursed Mr. Xander and every banker in a hundred-mile radius. "That's a very convenient thing to leave out when telling your clients about their debts," I snapped. "We can pay. Tomorrow. Or, here,"—I wrenched the stones from my pocket and held them out—"take these and I'll have another tomorrow."

Snake-smile eyed the gems and licked his lips, his greed turning to dismay. "Can't, miss. Sorry. Mr. Xander wants the payment brought to him in whole by one of your household. But come by tomorrow with your payment and we might be able to sort something out." He spat onto Charity's newly blossomed climbing roses and went back to shouting orders.

I yanked Mother's portrait out of the other man's hand. I wanted to give him a furious upbraiding, but Charity sagged against me. Crooning comforts, I led my baby sister inside, shoving past another man on his way out and forcing myself to ignore what he had plundered.

I had just settled Charity into bed, having seen two couches and a cabinet leave the house, when Father called for me.

"Beauty!"

It hardly sounded like him at all. But he appeared in Charity's doorway, his face pale with shock and anger, and the sinking in my belly told me that some of that anger was directed toward me.

"How dare you, *Bellezza*? My own daughter. Meddling with the fey?"

I had only ever seen him this angry once before, and it had frightened me then. Now I was dismayed but not cowed, and all I could think was how our home was being taken apart around our ears and all he could focus on was that I had disobeyed a rule that meant nothing now.

"I wasn't meddling, Father." I kept my voice even, clipped. "I was saving all of us."

"That was never your job!"

My eyes widened. The irony of the words, all I had done, all I had kept hidden—I could no longer tamp down my anger. Something snapped within me, loosening a red fury. "Whose was it then? Yours? Do you know how our finances were handled over the past few years? Because I do. I do, *Papà!* I have kept the records. I have used the skills you didn't want to acknowledge to keep us alive when you were too busy burying your head in the sand."

"*Non sai nulla.*" His voice was hoarse, bitter. Patience and Clotilde stood behind him, watching me with wide, worried eyes; in the distance someone shouted and a heavy crash of splintered wood made Patience glance heavenward.

"I was trying, too," he continued. "When you have known love like I have, Beauty, you will understand the loss I suffered, but are you thinking of others? You are only thinking of yourself and your cursed magic!"

My vision burst with red spots as Father's voice rose; I had never been so angry in my life. "I can't believe that even you could be so blind! My magic—my double alchemy— saved our lives after Mother died, and it's going to save us again. I have these four rubies"—I shuffled through my pockets and pulled out the gems—"duplicated by agreement with a fey prince. Tomorrow I'll duplicate the last and pay back our debts with the same magic you hate! But if you'll excuse me now, this is very troubling for all of us. I must take care of Charity."

"A fey prince?" Father blustered, and ran a trembling hand through his hair. "A fey prince. *I miei dei.*" His voice had gone quiet, and I had turned my back to him where Charity lay with red, streaming eyes, pleading silently with me.

But Father didn't see her. He erupted in a steady stream of curses in both languages, blaming me for betraying our family and courting the very thing that had destroyed us to begin with. I parried barb for barb. Such a lack of restraint inflamed a biting triumph burning within me.

"Stop it, both of you!"

Charity's voice cut through the melee. Her face blazed red with anger, her eyes glassy with tears. "That's enough! Just stop—"

She didn't finish her sentence before a deep racking cough shook her shoulders. I could hear Patience and Clotilde hurry away for some remedy or other, speaking in undertones, as if they knew, as if they'd expected—

Charity's eyes weren't glassy with tears but fever; my sense of triumph turned bitter and crumbled to ash. I'd hardly noticed in the summer afternoon heat and the fire of my own anger that my baby sister was terribly ill.

10. The Price

"Why didn't you tell me you were ill, sweet?"

I sat up with Charity, sponging one of Patience's brews across her forehead. She had slept for a few hours and woken bleary eyed and restless. Father had gone to bed after bringing up food for her; he looked sad, hurt, and small, but he said nothing to me, and I said nothing to him, more than happy to focus my efforts on tending my baby sister. Hours ago, Clotilde had given us each a gentle squeeze on the shoulder and went to bed. Patience was downstairs using our kitchen—the one room untouched—and I had yet to go to my own room, but I suspected I would find it empty and forlorn. Even Charity's bedroom held only her bed and a pile of clothes, hastily dumped on the floor when the armoire was taken.

"Why do you think?" Charity patted my hand. Her fever had broken, leaving a sheen of sweat on her skin and taking her strength, too, as if now that everyone knew about her illness she could stop pretending at last. When she spoke, her voice was more subdued than usual. "I've always been the baby, patted and coddled. I wanted to do something myself for once."

"Going to look for a job in your condition?" I frowned and shook my head. "You shouldn't endanger yourself like that."

98

She huffed, a very Charity sound. "There you go again. But look who's talking: Lowbridge. Lowbridge, my garden gloves. As if we thought the fey were less dangerous than illness. I knew something strange was going on with you. But you've always been so closed, so fiercely walled off and strong. You never really let us in, Beauty. And I knew if I told you I was seeking work, you and Patience would fuss and wheedle me into staying home. And I would let you do it. I'm not as strong as you are, but I want to make my own choices, the same as you."

"Oh, Charity." I felt guilt at her words, all the more because I had chided Armand for similar reasons only this morning. This morning seemed a lifetime away. I dragged my thoughts away from the castle and the fey prince who, even now, I missed with every fiber of my being. Charity's hand felt so small and frail when I took it in mine. She had a long scratch from one especially cantankerous fight with a thorn; otherwise, her hands were soft, as if all other rose bushes had sensed her sympathy and spared her their barbs. "I have underestimated you, haven't I?" I asked.

"Terribly. Just because you have magic that Father doesn't approve of doesn't make you better than the rest of us. We could all share our burdens, instead of making these furtive, solitary efforts."

I spent too much time squeezing the rag into the bowl, watching the herb-scented water splash and ripple.

"You've been trying to carry it all, haven't you?" she asked.

A few days ago I would have denied this with some offhand comment. Not anymore.

I nodded. "You're wiser than all of us, I think. We never spoke of what Father hated and feared; instead, we all went around him, rather than openly speaking of things, like you have."

"Yes. We went around you, too, sometimes. You can be very prickly, you know, and unapproachable when you think no one is paying attention."

"You have a lot of scolding to do for someone so ill," I chided, half in jest, but the humor fell flat. "Yes. Fine, I can be prickly. The world is harsh and I have always wanted to make my own way. But the world makes that very hard, too. You, my darling sister, this home—all of us—are everything I love best in the world. The only way I knew how to protect it all was through my own prickly, solitary way."

"If I am strong enough to make my own way," Charity said, "you might try being soft enough to let us help you."

I smiled. Armand's gentle chiding echoed in my sister's words to me, and I thought how much he and my sisters would enjoy one another's company, should they ever have met.

Charity began coughing again. She would go long minutes without it bothering her, but once it flared up, she struggled to subdue it. Every coughing fit left her weary and restless, and though she didn't say anything, her gentle eyes bore witness to pain.

After a while, when her breathing had calmed and she seemed to be asleep, I was about to go downstairs in search of our eldest sister when Charity whispered, "Father isn't angry at you, you know. He's angry at his own powerlessness."

"He made a fine job of convincing me otherwise," I replied softly.

"I know. And he shouldn't have, Beauty."

"No, he shouldn't have," said Patience, appearing in the doorway with a steaming bowl that smelled more pungent than the last. "I had words with him about it, too. He is to speak to you in the morning."

I looked at her incredulously. "You convinced him? Surely not to apologize. What potion did you threaten him with?"

My eldest sister sat down and began administering her brew to Charity by the spoonful. "Never you mind. Just make sure you only speak to him when you are ready to be sincere." The glance she gave me suggested that I should be just as sincere in my belief of her.

"I'm not surprised that you could persuade him, Patience, but you would uproot your entire garden and move it to the forest if it would please him."

"Oh, Beauty." There was that mildly condescending tone I knew; it almost made me smile, but it threatened to bring a lump to my throat. "I would never uproot my garden for Father. I wouldn't do it even for Laurine and she knows it. I only move the things I know I can. Most of the time," she had the good grace to acknowledge. In that moment I saw that I hadn't understood that about her. Of course Patience would fiercely guard what was truly hers, but she knew when to acquiesce and when to hold fast. I felt very childish again.

"What misfortune to be born between the world's most perfect sisters," I grumbled. "Pity me, kind ladies."

"Pity? More like endure," said Charity at the same time Patience said, "Of course we're perfect." We all laughed until Charity began coughing again.

"Time to rest," said Patience when the fit had passed. "You will go tomorrow to finish this task of yours, Beauty. We all know now. At least I can stop making that brew for you."

"Let me wait until the next day. You look exhausted," I protested, more from guilt than from a desire to put off my task, but Patience shook her head in her best big-sister, you-can't-win way.

"I took a few winks earlier when Clotilde prepared a late dinner. Go to sleep. Your bed is still there, though there's precious little else."

"They took hers," murmured Charity.

Patience glared at her reprovingly. "I'll sleep here, thank you. Now go, Beauty. You look more worn out than I feel."

I kissed Charity's forehead and embraced Patience, grateful for their presence, their forgiveness, and mostly for the fact that they were themselves. And with that relief, all my fatigue came crashing in on me.

"And Beauty," Charity murmured, "I am proud of you." I gave her a watery, grateful smile and carried her words with me as I stumbled into bed. I hardly noted the emptiness of my childhood room before sleep claimed me.

Drowsily, I reached for Armand, only to remember that I was alone. After tomorrow, I would never embrace him again.

He would return home. Had I never allowed myself to fall for him—had I hurried faster with the duplicating— maybe Charity would not have spent so much time out, and maybe she would never have fallen ill in the first place.

It is time for your payment.

The voice surrounded me in the dark. I didn't know where I was, whether I slept or woke, but a dreadful recognition of this voice and what it announced enveloped me. Whatever the cause of the delay, it had not forgotten, and its powers had not constrained it to that cursed graveyard. The spirit had found me after all.

"I must be allowed to choose it," I said, or thought, and the voice laughed.

The time for that is past, mortal. You did not claim the right when it was yours to claim. I choose.

"You gave me no time," I accused. "You took away my choice. You are to blame."

Is that so? You are the one who trespassed sacred ground—a move that wins my begrudging admiration—but there must be a price.

I fought to speak, to fight, to argue; anything to resist the growing fear that brought a terrible certainty of what would be taken.

What do you love most in all the world? Money? You already have gems, and you have the mark of magic on you. Your own magic, it would seem. I wonder how much it would pain you to lose these precious skills.

My magic? I felt a twinge of loss that quickly turned to relief. To escape with everything else—I could live without double alchemy. My desire to speak died, replaced with a prayer that the spirit would find its own suggestion sufficient.

Oh. But there is something else.

Cold fingers sorted through my soul. It was the only way I could describe the sensation, the feeling of being pulled apart piece by piece until every one of my deepest loves and truest fears were on display and my premature relief dissolved.

A sound—could it be a laugh?—breezed past my shoulder. *Love. Of course. I will take someone you love.*

No, no— "No piece of metal and stone is worth a person's life!"

Are you so sure? Then you do not understand what you stole. Your youngest sister, I wonder? Her life might suffice. Perhaps your oldest sister, in the prime of her youth? Or your father, growing older every day? Surely his time approaches. It would almost be a mercy.

Fear prickled down my limbs. The delight in its voice was real and sharp as thorns. "*Porca puttana!* You cannot do this!"

I must take someone.

It came to me then, the only plea I could make that would spare the lives of those I loved. It would crush me with the cost of its weight.

"Take Armand!" I cried.

Who is this Armand?

I was not fooled. Delight remained in the spirit's voice.

"You know who. You are more powerful than you seem. You want someone I love? Take Armand's feelings for me."

The words hung in the air as if weighed on some cruel, capricious scale.

"Taking someone does not have to mean taking their life," I gasped. "Take the prince's feelings for me, his memories of us, whatever you must do—but let him live."

Live?

"Leave his life untouched and separated from my own. I will never look for him. I will long for him and know that love for him will corrode my heart for the rest of my life while he forgets my very existence. But do not kill anyone, and leave my family alone." My voice broke. I had tried to sound fierce, but I was weary and heavy with despair.

Silence stretched, thin, cold, and cruel.

"Promise me!" I sobbed.

I am surprised, came the voice. *Humans will do anything foolish for those who warm their beds and fickle hearts. Instead you choose betrayal.*

"You must accept my choice!"

Surprised.

I woke reaching for Armand, needing to warn him, needing to beg his forgiveness. Tears soaked my pillow and crusted my skin with salt. But I could not and would not take back my plea. I cursed the spirit as its final words haunted me, burned into my mind like a gem that refused to bend to my will.

Humans will do anything foolish for those who warm their beds and fickle hearts.

11. Heart of Stone

Instead of entering the castle through the front doors, I veered off the gravel path and ran toward the open terrace where Armand and I had shared a late breakfast not long ago. I passed Gabriel and Daphne walking along a garden path bordered with summer's lush growth. We all exchanged a brief greeting, and though Gabriel looked about to say more, I hurried on through the garden. I wondered if everything would vanish the moment I duplicated the final stone, leaving me alone in an empty forest.

My heart gave a bruised leap when I saw Armand seated in the same chair as yesterday, writing on a piece of parchment and looking almost completely visible; the only difference was a faint blurring of his hands when he held the parchment up and gave it a shake. He jumped to his feet when he saw me and tossed the parchment on the table, running to enfold me in his arms. His kiss was slow and tender.

"Will you forgive me, Beauty?"

"For going home?" I said, spreading my hands across his chest. He nodded. "There is nothing to forgive, Armand, not from you." Something twisted inside me; it should have been a relief that he was preparing for our separation, that he had accepted it as inevitable and inescapable, and in my head I knew this. But my heart and body ached.

I looked up and held his gaze and prayed for forgiveness for how selfish I was. "But I want you one last time."

"I cannot refuse you." His words sent pangs of longing and regret through me. We ran inside to his bedroom, hungry for one another.

The world could have ended and we wouldn't have noticed. We lay tangled in his sheets afterward, and the way Armand's hand ran gently over my frizzed curls suggested he was committing every detail of me to memory, as I was of him. I shut my eyes and swallowed tears. My memories of him would follow me to my grave; a comfort and a curse all its own. A deep inhale left as a repressed sob.

"Beauty," he murmured, holding me tight. "You don't have to leave."

I lay there in silence, grappling with his words as a deepening dread crept through me, knowing he had mistaken the source of my grief.

"You know I have to," I began.

"No. Listen. You said this was temporary. But this—we need to last." He spoke in a whisper as if afraid his voice would shatter his own words. I shook my head. He gently lifted my face and looked me in the eye, but I turned away, unable to meet his gaze. "No, Beauty, listen," he pleaded. "Listen to me. If you don't want to stay, I understand. That was never part of our agreement. But I'm not asking you to stay so you can keep my bed warm. I am asking you to stay because I love you. I want you by my side and no one else."

"By your side?" I repeated stupidly. He loved me? "No, I don't understand—"

"I want you to be my wife and the princess of Clear Star, preferably in that order. You are wise and cunning and thoughtful and so brave and I would do anything, anything, do you understand, for you. You support me in a way no one else does. I want us to support each other. Let me be the one who cherishes and believes in you most in all the worlds."

"Armand, I can't." I brushed futilely at the tears spilling down my cheek and onto his chest. He reached up to wipe my tears with his thumbs.

"Is it your family?" His brown eyes were earnest, thoughtful and searching. "You would hate to leave them, and you have all suffered so much. They would be more than welcome to live here; I would make sure they never lack for anything. I know we could win your father over; how could he not be happy to see you happy? Or, if they prefer to stay in your current home, I will still make certain they would remain comfortable. Should others prove unkind toward them for your connection with me, I would do anything within my power—"

"Stop." I pushed away from him and sat up, swinging my legs over the side of the bed so I didn't have to see the damage I was about to wreak upon him.

Until that moment, I hadn't thought he truly loved me; it was the one thing that gave me a tiny measure of comfort, believing that the spirit would not take something of great significance to him. I thought we shared a heated passion, understanding that what we had was fleeting, and here he was declaring his love for me—love!—and offering me all the things I wanted most. He even made the thought of marriage appealing; a partnership where death, more powerful than any spirit, always takes one and leaves the other to grieve alone. Alone, we were powerful. Together, we could be formidable. He was offering to share all the space between now and death, a partnership of intimate vows.

But I had paid a price that could not be undone. Foolishly, I had thought the graveyard spirit's demands were brittle, easily escaped. How wrong I was.

"Armand." I shut my eyes; speaking the words felt like extracting a dagger from my side, yet he deserved the truth. "I told you where I found the necklace. But I never told you at what cost." I swallowed. The mattress shifted; I could feel him sitting beside me, waiting. "A spirit guarding the necklace demanded something in return. I—it took you."

The silence was worse than any nightmare. When Armand spoke, his voice was sharp, wary. "What does that mean?"

"It demanded someone I love as payment. Tried to take my family, would have killed them, I don't know—but I asked it to separate us. You and me. To spare your life but keep us apart. We have no future together." My mind raced. I searched his face, pleading silently, but his eyes were fixed ahead, his jaw working.

"What you are telling me," he said, his voice so odd and detached that he sounded like a stranger, "is that I have no choice regarding our future at all."

"What was I supposed to do?" Hurt gave my words barbs. "Armand, what of your fey codes? I have my own, and they are just as important, because they protect people I love. You have no right to tell me to give up my family!"

"You should have told me of this spirit to begin with!" Armand burst out. "Did you not think I could have done something to help—"

"I have my pride." My throat burned with unshed tears. "How could I have demanded that you, a stranger, a prince, pay the price for something that I had chosen?"

"But you did, Beauty. I am paying. You kept it to yourself and now this—" He leapt from the bed and pulled on his clothes. He ran his hands through his hair, a frantic, helpless gesture, and exhaled roughly. As if to himself, he said, "No. What else could you have done?" He strode to the other side of the bed. "I wish you had trusted me and let me help you. Gods, Beauty. A stranger? Is that what you think of me still?"

"No! The spirit demanded something of great value. Someone I love."

With this terrible admission, Armand's eyes filled with pain that felt like my own.

"I didn't think you loved me," I whispered.

His face hardened. He bent to gather something.

"What are you doing?" I asked. When he came to me, I reached to embrace him. Instead, he placed my clothes on my lap.

"I'll take you to the necklace when you're dressed."

"Armand!"

He turned at the door, his eyes full of hurt.

I searched for a way to ease his pain, now inextricably linked to my own. "I don't know if the spirit will take your love for me, your memories of us, or something else, but—"

"Don't worry about me," he interrupted. "It doesn't matter. Either way, soon it will be as if nothing happened between us." He turned so I could no longer see his expression. "I'm sorry I caused you pain by expressing my love. I had no idea it was worth so little."

"Armand!" I called after him, but he was gone.

I was wrong about the loss of him crushing me. As I sat dazed and crying, a terrible, empty loneliness left me hollow instead.

Tristan escorted me to the terrace where Armand stood stiff and formal. The councillor looked between the two of us but said nothing.

"Here, Beauty." Tristan handed me the charmed bracelet Armand had first made for me. "The whole council, especially Gabriel, reworked the spell to add a traveling charm. When this castle disappears, it will allow you to return home safely."

I took it numbly, nodding. Tristan gave me a sympathetic look. He stepped back so Armand stood before me, leaving no way for us to avoid parting words.

"Thank you for your assistance." The prince spoke formally, as if we had never met. I wondered if his memories, love, or both were already bleeding away. I lifted my chin to meet his gaze, but he glanced down at the necklace. "We hope your double alchemy provides adequate recompense for your efforts, and send you with the goodwill of the fey."

"Goodwill sounds unnecessary, since I will never darken your threshold again," I said, despite my better judgment. Armand's face did not change.

I wasted no more time. Magic poured through my fingers, a partial distraction from the pain swirling in my heart. Whether it was because of this pain or the weakened curse, I experienced almost none of the usual negative effects.

The final *plink* sounded like the last strike on a nail in the fragile casket of something that had withered before it could bloom. Armand and the gems faded from my mind's eye. The cursed prince was free.

A sound like the rush of wind surrounded me. My eyes snapped open to see the exiled fey castle fading like mist in the morning sun, and a gaping, fragile hole seemed to reopen in my heart. The prince of Clear Star was still visible. His stoic expression faded to confusion, and he cried out words I couldn't hear. Then he was ghostlike, ephemeral. Armand, and everything, everyone else, vanished.

I stood alone in the forest holding a handful of precious stones as cold as the cavity in my chest.

12. After the Price is Paid

There is something to be said for diverting grief into anger. Instead of going home first, I stormed into Larkspur Bank, demanded an audience with Mr. Xander, and without waiting, burst into his office. His eyes widened at the sight.

"This will pay for our debts, will it not?" I set each stone on his desk with precision. The banker blathered and blustered, so I continued. "I will wait at home for your men to return our belongings." I leaned forward over the desk. "And if I find one table leg dented, a single page torn, you, sir, are the one who will need to sort things out, and I mean compensate us to the last penny."

I left Mr. Xander surprised and sputtering a promise to see to everything, and marched home in a righteous triumph.

How blessedly quiet our home was this time. I smiled with grim satisfaction, imagining the same scoundrels who had stolen our things now bearing their loads with contrite—or at least sullen—expressions. Clotilde met me at the front door, worry deepening the lines on her face.

"I'm sorry, Beauty," she said, and there was something wrong in her voice. My relief slipped away as cold fingers gripped my heart.

Without waiting for her to elaborate, I ran inside and pounded up the stairs to Charity's door. There was no sound from within the quiet room. I flung open the door.

She was alone, lying in her bed. Her chest rose and fell in a gentle rhythm.

Breathing. Asleep. Alive.

I sank beside her on the bed and sobbed.

Moments later, the mattress sagged as my eldest sister joined me.

"There, Beauty, my dearest." Patience's hands gently rubbed my arms until I leaned against her and cried like a baby. I cried because my sister was alive and I cried because the man I loved was gone, and there was no double alchemy or fey magic in the world that could take me back to the time before I had known death or romantic love and their cruel losses, when my only concern was whether or not I would best the next cocky boy at Ward. How long ago that time seemed.

"Oh." Patience stroked my hair, humming as if she were the mother and I the child. "You really love him. You poor lamb."

"I'm being childish." I sat up and wiped my nose on my sleeve. "Charity is well. That's enough tears from me. Besides, how did you know? I never said anything."

There, the condescending look. "Laurine wasn't the first woman I loved. I know heartache when I see it. You're not being childish, dearest. Oh, Beauty, my poor Beauty. On top of everything else."

I looked down when Charity's frail hand patted ours. "I'm feeling better," she whispered, not convincingly, "so Father has a chance, too."

"What?" I glanced from Charity's wan face to Patience's wary one. "What do you mean?"

My father had never been ill my entire childhood, not even at his lowest moments of grief, at least in body. Now he looked flushed with fever but also pale and diminished.

Clotilde stood up from the chair where she sat sponging his forehead with a cool compress.

"When did it start?" I asked, wishing I had seen him this morning before leaving for the castle. How I regretted not speaking to him earlier, as Patience had prompted.

"Only this morning. He was preparing to leave the house, but when he mentioned how his eyes hurt, Patience hurried him into bed."

"Charity is feeling better," I said with a hopefulness I did not feel.

"Yes. It's been going through the town, the butcher says. A dozen or so have died already and they were only sick a day or so." She glanced up with fear in her eyes, as if worrying she had said the wrong thing.

"But Charity is feeling better," I repeated. "Some will recover. They will recover, they must. And this is not the same fever that took my mother, Clotilde, so let's not even think of that."

"Of course not." Clotilde shook her head.

"Nadia?" Father stirred, Mother's name on his tongue. His eyes opened slowly. "Nadia, don't leave me again."

"Father, you're here in your own home, with Clotilde and me, and Charity and Patience nearby," I said, fighting to keep my voice steady. Even with his eyes open, his gaze was unfocused as he searched the ceiling for something we couldn't see. I took his hand in mine. It was warm and dry, like fallen leaves.

"It's your daughter, Beauty," Clotilde said. "Your daughters need you."

"Need me?" Still his voice sounded frail. "They haven't needed me for a long time, Nadia. I should have been there more. But I wanted to follow you after you left. You wouldn't let me."

Clotilde and I exchanged a watery glance as I pushed down the lump in my throat. "Father, I know you're angry at me because I used my magic. But I had to. I paid for our house. We don't have to leave. I forgot to tell Patience and Charity." I gave a snuffling laugh. "We can't afford to be ladies of luxury, but the work will be good for us. They'll be so happy. I did what I had to, just as you have, just as we all have. If you're still going to be angry at me, you'll have to be angry at all of us, and we both know you're too softhearted for that."

Nothing but silence followed this. I ached to know he heard me. When I tried again, my voice broke. "*Papà*, do you know I paid a price, too?"

He became fretful, muttering and stirring. Clotilde continued to sponge cool water on his skin and muttered her own urgings.

"Bellezza." His eyes closed, but his voice sounded more stable. "Beauty, are you well?"

"Yes," I sniffed. "No, Father."

He sighed deeply, opened his eyes, and looked at me.

"Don't be ashamed, *mia figlia*," he said, and his eyelids fluttered shut and the final exhale left his lungs.

Grief is as cruel as love, for we wouldn't know one without the other. Everyone talks about how love expands and grows stronger; no one says that grief does the same. That it swells in waves until you grow tired of fighting and wish to drown. But unlike the sea, grief mocks you by keeping you alive, never giving you the relief of unconsciousness, even in sleep.

The next morning brought the perfect summer day. Patience and I flung open Charity's bedroom windows, where the climbing roses nodded and sent their fragrance in like a blessing, and though the grief of losing Father lay heavy upon us, we felt the strength of our sisterhood offering some sweetness amidst the bitter.

I read aloud while Patience mended Father's best shirt. Neither said anything when I stopped and cried every few pages, as they were crying too, and Charity held my hand. Laurine had just brought the news that carts were rolling down the road toward us with our furniture and was downstairs waiting with Clotilde.

"You'll be outside again soon, talking to your flowers, Sweet," I said. But Charity's hand had grown still.

I have little memory of what happened next. I think Patience screamed for Father, or Laurine. I don't remember if the shell of my baby sister looked pale, or agitated, or beautiful. I wish the gentle, serene beauty of the day felt as if it were just for her, that the thought somehow made her departure easier. I wish I could say the end of her suffering brought some relief. But it did not.

Our youngest sister was gone. The shock of her sudden absence made no sense at all.

My sweet, sweet Charity.

Grief is as cruel as love.

13. A Chance for Love

Laurine glanced up from her teacup. "Sell the house?"

We had just come back from the funeral, held in the town's rolling, green graveyard with its ordinary gravestones as still as the dead. Multiple fresh graves adorned the expanse; our town had seen many casualties over the past few weeks. Patience, Laurine, Clotilde, and I sat in the small parlor where we held cups of tea, largely forgotten.

"Beauty and I agreed, and Clotilde wants to go home to her daughter's." Patience leaned against Laurine while her love rubbed her arm.

"This house is too big for the three of us." I looked at the furniture, all of which had been returned to this room. We'd burned two mattresses and sold their frames, and none of their other personal furniture had come back, a fact none of us had the heart to contest. My Ward game had gone to the tavern, where the keeper gave me more than a fair price for it so we could pay the funeral expenses. The large parlor was as bare as a stripped bone and even our favorite room felt hollow as a shell. I felt the same disoriented fogginess in this room that I did every day now, having to stop myself from asking several times why Father or Charity hadn't joined us yet and thinking that I should go drag her in from the sweetly scented garden. The truth was that I couldn't bear to stay here, where memories haunted worse than ghosts and demanded more from me than I could give. I looked down at my tea, now cold, and swirled the contents in the cup.

Patience and Laurine were locked in a secret whisper battle, judging by the raise of Patience's eyebrows and the tilt of Laurine's chin. "Out with it, you two," Clotilde demanded.

"You see? I told you to wait," protested Patience.

Sensing the topic of their discussion, I said, "You both finally decided to get married? Wonderful. It's about time."

Laurine blinked at me while Clotilde smiled. "This is not the time," Patience began, but I could tell she was at war with herself. "We had agreed to wait at least until spring, but—"

"It's the perfect time," I insisted.

"Here, here," added Clotilde.

"If anything, the earlier the better. We need some happy news. And life is too brief to wait for important things."

Laurine flew across the room and kissed me on both cheeks, throwing "I told you so" over her shoulder to Patience, who was crying both for grief and joy since the only time she could cry at all was when she felt at least two conflicting emotions at once.

And here we are, I thought, as the three women began talking about the wedding with an enthusiasm real enough to promise future joy.

I didn't want life to go on. But it did all the same.

And somehow, I had to push through my overwhelming guilt and loneliness and move on as well.

Patience and Laurine married on a crisp, mellow day between summer and autumn. Soon after, we sold our house and most belongings that remained. We saw Clotilde off to her daughter's, promising to visit her, and carefully transplanted as many of the herbs and roses from our old garden as possible.

"So you would move your garden for Laurine after all," I teased Patience. With her share of the sale she had purchased a small lot behind Laurine's smithy, where the three of us were digging up the soil and replanting our small host of green things.

Patience ignored me while Laurine laughed.

"We'll save enough to build a little place of our own on this plot soon," Laurine said, wiping her forehead and leaving a streak of dirt. She gestured to the smithy, not ten yards away. "Close enough to work and Patience's garden. She's getting a reputation for being the best herb witch in town—yes you are, darling, stop acting so modest. You'd be more than welcome to stay with us then, too, Beauty. We'll have a larger home."

Patience echoed the sentiment, and I smiled. While I loved my sister and her wife, the past few weeks had been cramped living above the smithy. And I was feeling restless. I had no need to practice double alchemy at the moment and felt no desire to. That should have made me sad, but like so many things, it just left me feeling hollow. Still, another old love whispered to me, and I had some desire to answer that call.

"Thank you," I said. "But I've heard that the Ward group from our town is traveling, and there's to be a tournament in Green Hill soon. It's time to show those men what they missed out on by rejecting me from their little group." I looked up to see Patience studying me with the concern of a big sister. There were a dozen things she wanted to say and her expression said them all, but true to her namesake, she waited for me to speak. "Can I still stay with you when I return?" I asked.

Both women replied enthusiastically in agreement. Then, as Laurine returned to her task, my sister asked the dreaded question. "What will you do about Armand?"

I shook my head, pretending to examine a shademint stem. "He's forgotten me, or moved on by now, as I told you. There is nothing to do about him."

"Beauty," she said gently, pulling the plant from my hands. I stared at it, unwilling to meet her eyes. "It isn't like you to give up so easily, not on something that matters so much. Promise me you won't give up just yet. Or I might have to douse you with an unexpected potion." She smiled gently and went back to planting.

I joined them, but my mind was full of thoughts, as tender and easily bruised as new herbs. All these months I had refused to let myself think too much of Armand. A terrible fear that I had bargained away the life of my father, sister, or Armand—maybe all of them—clung to the corners of my consciousness like ghosts. They haunted my dreams with their pleas and rage, demanding to know what I had done. But every morning, I rose listening for Patience's voice and heard it. She was present, and she had a chance at happiness, and she loved me. She had helped me at her own risk. So I had kept busy for her sake. It hadn't been difficult with the funeral, the house, and the wedding commanding our time. But those events were now past. I stood in a new garden with nothing more pressing than Ward competitions, and those had lost their allure just moments after promising me a way of escape. I could not ignore Armand, or my love for him, any longer.

I needed answers, no matter how condemning they may be. Only one place offered a chance to lay my past to rest. And might I discover if my desire for a future with him, small and foolish yet stubborn enough to survive, had any chance of coming to fruition?

My doubts were no longer a valid excuse. It was time to seek the truth.

The fey graveyard was as strange as before. Gravestones twisting and contorting into strange shapes as I struggled my way back to the bloodred stone.

Greedy, just as I said. Immediately, the distorted voice swirled around me. *What now? Looking for more jewels?*

The hairs on my neck lifted. "I need to know," I said, breathless lest this spirit flee before answering my questions. "I need to know who you took from me."

I felt a curl of air around me, and something cold brushed against my hair.

So demanding for a mortal. Why should I answer you?

"Because I deserve to know." I struggled to maintain the confidence in my voice. "After all, I have your begrudging admiration."

A pause. *You are afraid.*

"I am. I am terrified that I have cost loved ones their lives. But that didn't stop me from seeking you out a second time, seeking the truth even if it condemns me. If you ever loved anyone—anyone at all—tell me. Did you really take Armand's love for me?"

What if I told you that I took nothing at all? A cold blast of wind surrounded me and I fought to stay upright as the voice tore at me. *What if I told you that it was you who destroyed Armand's love?* The spirit's warped voice was a chorus speaking as one, voices tangling together. Then the chorus unraveled, diminishing into the words of a single person.

Suddenly all was silent. In the quiet graveyard, a solitary figure stood before me.

She was a woman who might have been my age, though her sharp cheekbones and pointed ears suggested a number of differences. Pale blonde hair fell in curtains down her back. She wore a guarded, resigned expression on her beautiful face, a face whose mask of haughtiness looked tired and worn. "You are entirely too predictable," she said in an imperious voice. "I knew you would return. The man I cursed has returned to his country, as you witnessed. Yes, you needn't gawk," she went on, no doubt seeing surprise and recognition on my face. "Such an act of power as I performed left me much diminished. I fled to the nearest source of residual fey magic until I regained myself. And now that we've had this lovely chat, I've got other things to see to." Swifter than a swallow, she turned her back and receded into the trees.

"Wait!" I called out when she—Princess Soline—neared the graveyard's edge. "Is he happy?" When she did not answer, I began to fear a new truth. "Why did you let me have the necklace if it would free him from your curse? I'd have thought you'd want him to suffer for eternity. Does he suffer now?"

"I never expected a human to break my curse." A note of bitterness receded from Princess Soline's voice. "You'll excuse me if I keep what dignity I have left."

Torn between anger and a growing sense of hopelessness, I nonetheless drew a deep breath before speaking. Though her refined, court-trained exterior remained, I recognized something of myself in this woman. We had both loved with no chance of a happy ending. We had both gone to great lengths to get what we wanted, and both of us had paid heavy prices.

"Princess Soline—"

"I no longer claim that title."

"I love him," I began, mustering all my compassion. "You love him still, I think. I only want to know how he fares."

She gave a little shrug. "He is busy. Many changes have taken place since their return." Suddenly a crack in her imperious visage appeared. Soline's eyes grew large and shone with tears.

"He is miserable," she said, her voice small. "Armand thinks of you nearly every waking minute. Yes, I saw him in person," she said, answering my unspoken question and waving her hand. "No, I will not tell you about it, except to say that the man is quite out of his mind with missing you."

A hundred longings, fears, and questions flooded me. "Why are you admitting this?"

"First you demand to know, then you question my motives?" She raised an eyebrow and sighed. "Though my diminished powers tied me to the graveyard, I could occasionally cast my sight in search of where my necklace had gone. I had to watch helplessly as you fell in love with him."

"How much did you see?" I stuttered, my cheeks growing flushed.

She raised an eyebrow. "More than enough. When at last I could contact you, I tormented you with the threat of loss. I wanted you both to suffer as I had. But now . . ." Her face shifted back to resignation. "I decided to tell you the truth because I still love him and I do not want him to suffer any longer."

Already I was scanning the trees as if a doorway to Clear Star would open up before me, thoughtless elation buoying me up. I stopped myself from dashing away.

"I hardly deserve to ask. But how can I find him?"

"No doors will open to the country of Clear Star," Princess Soline said. "Mortals must be summoned or taken. But this will help."

I leapt to take the familiar necklace in her hand. When I relieved her of it, she withdrew her hand with a slight wince. From the weight and feel of the warm gold in my hands down to the crack down the largest ruby, it was unmistakably the same one she had relinquished to me only months ago. It offered no answers within its bloodred depths. But Armand was right: I thrived on challenge.

"What will you do?" I found myself asking.

She pondered the question with a frown. "I am forbidden from entering the kingdom, naturally. I may take up a humble occupation somewhere in the woods. Who can say? Now," she said briskly, squaring her shoulders, "summon him. Hold it to your heart and repeat his name three times. Prince Armand will answer you as he never answered me. And Beauty," she said, her voice sharp with warning, "you had better deserve him." She turned and walked to the edge of the graveyard and the stones shifted and transformed into their terrible shapes again. I could not tell when the former princess of Clear Star left the place behind for good, only that she was gone.

I wasted no time in performing the actions as instructed. But there is little to tell: nothing happened.

Again and again I tried to summon Armand, and still he did not appear. Desperate, I tried every variation of Soline's instructions that I could think of. But as I sat in that graveyard while afternoon melted into twilight, and the forest became dim with night, my elation curdled into bitter defeat. If he was truly miserable for want of me, why did he not respond? Had Soline tricked me yet again?

I was too tired to fear my surroundings. Curling up on a bed of soft moss, I shut my eyes and fell into a troubled sleep.

14. A New Magic

I sat at a table in Green Hill's cobblestone town square scattered with orange, red, and gold-leaved trees. A large crowd surrounded the table where we played. This was my fourth game of the day and my eleventh in five days; many Ward players had traveled to compete in the autumn games, and many more had come to watch. The amount of gold I'd already amassed jingled satisfactorily in my pockets, but this was the game I had waited for. For though I easily recognized the arrogant certainty on my current opponent's face and knew it was about to change, I recognized something else as well.

Sitting across from me was Gerbaud Chevalier, the very boy who had once dared me to enter the fey graveyard and fled it in panic. And he did not yet recognize me.

We played the game. Every now and then he would look at his companions and chuckle knowingly, while they grinned and urged him on. I kept my face neutral. When I landed the winning move, I smiled my first true smile in days.

"Had enough, Gerbaud? Or will you challenge me to a race in the fey graveyard? I can show you the necklace I found there, if you like."

Dazed recognition dawned on his face, and I laughed outright. My opponent stuttered, protested, and left the table, only to have the facilitator remind him to pay me my winnings. I smiled at his dismayed team, who backed into the crowd, and returned to counting my coins. A shadow fell across the table. I could afford to let my new opponent sweat for a minute.

"I would like to see that necklace."

"You shall have to wait, I'm afraid," I responded, then recognized the voice and looked up.

"I'll play you for it," said the prince of Clear Star, late afternoon sunlight haloing the brown hair that covered his fey ears and making him look like some ridiculous god from a tale. His expression was earnest. Looking at him felt like every time I had looked into his eyes; it brought back every time we had held each other close. My face warmed and the breath left my lungs.

He sat down without breaking eye contact. "You didn't pay the fee," I squeaked.

"Do you accuse me of cheating?"

Though Armand's face remained neutral, his voice rough with emotions. Which ones, I wasn't sure, but I *was* sure the crowd could hear the pounding of my heart.

"There are several things I could accuse you of," I replied. "Cheating isn't one of them."

Silently Armand paid the fee, and the moderator announced the start of the game.

We played silently at first. I remained rigid in my seat, watching his hand move to avoid searching his face.

"I've missed you."

Armand's words were so soft I almost thought I'd misheard him.

Click. I moved a piece, pain and uncertainty bristling like a porcupine in my heart and prodding me to speak sharply. "I've been busy."

Click. "So I see."

"Did Soline visit you after the spell broke? I met her, you know. She and I might have been friends. She seems impressive." *Click.*

"Beauty, I—"

"I hope she finds her new life satisfactory, but I doubt the scope will suit her. She will miss her old power."

"And you?" His voice had an edge to it. *Click.* "Do you miss your old power? Because I hardly believe that playing Ward is enough to satisfy someone with your fire and steel." He paused, sighed, and rubbed his temples. "I'm sorry; that was uncalled for. I have a reason for speaking to you."

"Oh?" I feigned disinterest, my heartbeat returning to a gallop. Why was he here now, and not when I had summoned him weeks ago? His reason, I thought, had better be a good one.

"We have decided we are in need of a council member who understands humans, and naturally, Tristan suggested you."

I blinked at him, stunned, still trying to understand if the bitterness in his voice earlier had been love or hate when the significance of his request sank in. "He can't be serious."

"He is. A lot has happened in the past few months. We want to better fey-human relations and we need someone who is human if we're to take that seriously. I am here to offer a formidable woman a position worthy of her power, if she will accept it."

He was right about Ward. I had bested my old enemy, and while I still loved the game, it did not provide the intellectual interaction I craved, the kind I had once found with a shadowed prince who saw through me in a way no one else had before or since. But this sudden request, and its magnitude, made it difficult for me to speak or even think clearly.

"And it would mean so much to me if I could see you." He spoke softly again, causing my uncertainty to protest even louder.

"You're seeing me now." *Clack.* I set the piece down with more force than necessary. "And if that's so, then why didn't you come when I summoned you?"

He looked confused. "What do you mean?"

"This necklace." I took it from the pouch and held it up, noting the surprise on Armand's face. Soline had come to me after returning to Clear Star. Had she said nothing of the necklace to Armand? Had she stolen it back? "What other necklace did you think you were asking to see, when we began this game? She said I could summon the prince of Clear Star with it. I tried. And you didn't come."

"I wasn't really thinking about a necklace," he admitted quietly. "I wanted to hear you speak to me. And I'm not the prince of Clear Star anymore."

It was my turn to be surprised. "What?"

"After Tristan's rest, the council voted him to be the prince. I agreed to step down for him. Holding the foremost position at court is not the only way to help my people—not the best, in fact, for me or them. So." He exhaled, glancing warily at me. "The necklace could not summon me because I am no longer the prince."

I stared at him, my hand suspended over the game. "And Tristan didn't see fit to mention that I had summoned you?"

"The magic does not work like that. It must be connected to both name and title. Soline wouldn't have known I was no longer prince because it happened after she left. She must have taken the necklace without my noticing it." He glanced down and plucked a piece from the board, spinning it between his fingers. "I haven't stopped thinking about you, Beauty. There were many responsibilities to see to. I could not intrude on you, either. I thought you would not want that."

My heart leapt, tumbled, and fell as I remembered his last words to me, the stiff formality with which he had spoken. After all that had passed between us it felt unfair, unjust even, that he should be here speaking tender things to me that left bruises more exquisite than any conscious torment. I had hurt him too, yet here he was.

I inhaled slowly. "And what do you want, Armand?"

"At first, in truth, not simply to leave you in peace. It hurt that you chose for me, even though the other choices available to you were egregious. I thought I could have—should have—helped you make a better choice. I could have fought with this spirit." He shook his head. "It was never my choice to make."

"Your time is almost done," said the moderator, nodding at the large sand clock where black particles trickled into a cone of lost time. There was shuffling and murmuring throughout the crowd.

"I believe you love me," Armand said. Certainty blazed in his eyes and made my breath catch. "The spirit had demanded someone you loved. I was hurt and acted the fool, thinking that if you truly loved me, you would never have made your choice."

He paused, his eyes searching, full of regret. The cold space in my heart began to warm.

"Go on," I urged.

"Whatever decision you make is yours and yours alone. I understand why you acted the way you did, and it does not hurt anymore. But I will hurt if you don't speak to me. I'm sorry it took me so long to find you. I have no excuse for that, because I know you love me and still it took me all these months to find the courage to risk losing you a second time. To tell you again that I love you and want to marry you."

My heart hammered. Here was Armand, not as I had encountered him during our first meeting, hiding behind clever words and shadows. Here was a man baring himself as naked as if we lay together in bed.

There were too many eyes on us, and I was afraid. But the time we had left, the time we might share, was suddenly infinitely more important than all the Ward games of all the worlds. There were many outcomes possible in Ward. There was only one outcome for us that I wanted.

I spoke before any of my fears could break the surface. "Can you still transport us?"

Armand stood and held out his hand. I rose, leaped to close the distance between us, jostling the board, and clasped my arms around him.

The last thing I heard was the scattering of Ward pieces against the cobblestones, and the last thing I saw was Armand's brown eyes fixed on me.

When the fey kingdom of Clear Star appeared around me I thought we had entered an enchanted night. An indigo sky resolved into hundreds of midnight blue rooftops, all scattered with what appeared to be the incandescent light of stars. Even the cobblestones gleamed like silver. Something told me we were near the castle, but it was all so disorienting and beautiful until Armand's nearness overwhelmed all of that and cast it into shadow. We kissed as if to make up for lost time.

When we broke apart, I buried my face in the crook of his neck and wept, allowing my fears to surface at last, rising like the unquiet dead in search of some unfinished task.

"I do love you," I said through my tears. "I want to choose us."

He began rubbing my back in slow, soothing circles. "But?" he prompted gently.

"But I don't know if we can be together."

"Your family."

"My father and younger sister are gone. I tried so hard to save them, Armand, but I couldn't save them from death. Sometimes I feel as though I've killed them, no matter what I tell myself. And I'm not sure I feel worthy of happiness."

He exhaled deeply, as if my burden was his, and kissed my forehead. For a while he held me and stroked my hair as I wept. Gradually, a sense of comfort suffused me, strong enough to make me believe that one day I might release this sense of blame for good.

"I'm so sorry," he whispered. "You've had more than your share of suffering, Beauty. I'm so sorry I wasn't there for you." He sighed again; his chest rose and fell beneath me, a soothing, beguiling rhythm I wanted to feel for the rest of my life. "I'm not sure I feel worthy of happiness, either. We hurt those we love the most, and those who love us are cheated. None of life seems fair."

I patted my tear-stained cheeks and nose with a sleeve and looked him in the eye. He had come to find me. He was with me, real and warm and comforting. "Alone, we are powerful," I said. "Yet together, we would be formidable. Life is too short to wait on important things. Armand, I accept."

He rubbed my arms, smiling incredulously. "The position, or my hand?"

"Does becoming a council member entail calming emotionally volatile men? Because if so, then I refuse the position."

He bent his head, exhaling into my hair. "Not in the way you experienced it, Beauty," he said, chuckling with relief. "In all truthfulness, I cannot guarantee that it will never occur as part of the job, but you would not have to handle it alone. No one has ever been so troublesome as Gabriel when he was afflicted. And you would find him one of your staunchest allies, if you took the position."

"And you? What is your position now, former Prince Armand?"

I hadn't meant to sound suggestive, but the gleam in his eyes told me he had something other than politics in mind. "Have you forgotten? I am also part of the council," he said, the corners of his mouth twitching in a smile, "and I am waiting to know if I might have the pleasure of marrying one of my fellow council members."

"That depends." I plucked at his collar. "Have you asked Gabriel? He was very keen to offer himself as a husband once, and you—"

I broke off with a shriek of laughter as Armand nibbled my neck. "It serves me right, I suppose," he murmured against my skin. He straightened and held my gaze. "Beauty, I want to work by your side as fellow servants of the people, to be your greatest support and to love you best in all the worlds. Will you marry me?"

"Such formalities from a councilman." I put my hand on his cheek and smiled. "I promise to remind you that you are worthy of help when you forget it and scold you when you are self-righteous. I promise to share my burdens with you and not carry them all alone. And yes, Armand, I accept your hand and a seat on the council, in that order."

Armand's smile shone bright as the light of Clear Star, and we gathered each other into a passionate kiss.

There are many kinds of magic in this world, and much they can and cannot do. There may always be some ghosts that never fully leave us. Yet what Armand and I create together—fey and human, body and soul, cleverness and love, and yes, fire and steel—is the richest kind of magic I know.

Acknowledgements

I'd like to thank my editor, Jessica Allowski of Cozy Cottage Editing, for being such a steady, gentle, and affirming support of this book and of me.

Thank you to Bethany Stedman, who is always keen to read my stories, offer feedback, and share my excitement.

To all my beta readers, Lynden, Poorvi, Lydia, Ami, Rhiannon, and Courtney, thank you for spending your time with Beauty and Armand before they were ready to head out into the world. Your input made a big difference.

Thank you to Vera Lee, Jess Lynn, Beth, Keturah, Missy, Laura, Jennifer, Lydia, Evangeline, Kieran, Angelika, and Sylvia for being an ARC reader and for hyping my book up. I'm so grateful for every one of your reviews.

A lot of wonderful people I've connected with through Instagram and my newsletter spread the word and cheered me on. Thank you for your support. You are the best.

To my sisters, I heart you so much. I'm sorry about Charity. Don't be like her, k?

To my kids, as I write 'another book'. You're super cool.

To Mike, for your stability and for making me laugh. We make some pretty good magic, don't we?

Finally, thank you for reading this book. I couldn't do this without you.

Also by Stephanie Ascough

A Land of Light and Shadow
Upper middle-grade fantasy novel for grown-ups & kids

Flower and Cloak
Five fairy tales for the curious, romantic, and deep-feeling
souls

The Wistful Wild
Fairy tale poems of longing and ferocity

Twisted Halls
Clear Star Romance 2
Release date TBA

Looking for more? Check out Riona Beck, the author's pen
name imprint dedicated to sweet, open-door romance
inspired by folklore and fairy tales, and be the first to know
when these books (and more) will be released:
Rionabeck.com

Crystalline
Ella and Rodan~crumbling English estate circa 18th
century~virgin/'playboy'~Cinderella/Frog Prince
vibes/humorous and sweet

Silver Waves
Mirren and Flynn~Scottish folklore inspired~forced
proximity~only one bed/melancholic and sensual

RIONA
BECK

About the Author

Stephanie Ascough (she/her) is a neurodivergent writer who loves folklore and fairy tales. She is the author of several books, as well as poems and short stories in other publications.

When she isn't writing or researching her latest special interest, you can find her reading, avoiding housework, or exploring the Appalachian Mountains of Tennessee, where she lives with her husband, four children, and assorted cats/fae (none of whom are related to the fey in this book). Connect with her on Instagram @author.stephanieascough, or through her newsletter, The Purple Vale, on Substack (purplevale.substack.com).

www.ingramcontent.com/pod-product-compliance
Lightning Source LLC
Chambersburg PA
CBHW051958170626
46808CB00007B/2683